Praise for the Raine Stockton Dog Mysteries

Rapid Fire

"Rich with depictions of North Carolina's beautiful Smoky Mountains, Ball's latest is a cozy with a hint of romance. Raine Stockton is a delightful protagonist, a very human, down-to-earth character. As she quickly becomes immersed in a well-crafted mystery, she's forced to choose between the only two men she's ever loved—a sheriff and a fugitive." —*Romantic Times*

"There can't be too many golden retrievers in mystery fiction for my taste." —*Deadly Pleasures*

Smoky Mountain Tracks

"[A] twisty tale, a riveting finale, and a golden retriever to die for." —Carolyn Hart

"[*Smoky Mountain Tracks*] has everything—wonderful characters, surprising twists, great dialogue. Donna Ball knows dogs . . . the Smoky Mountains . . . [and] how to write a page-turner. I loved it." —Beverly Connor

"[A] story of suspense with humor and tenderness." —Carlene Thompson

"[Ball] ting and provden whodunilik-able, dediew

Other books in the
Raine Stockton Dog Mystery Series

Smoky Mountain Tracks
Rapid Fire

GUN SHY

A Raine Stockton Dog Mystery

Donna Ball

A SIGNET BOOK

SIGNET
Published by New American Library, a division of
Penguin Group (USA) Inc., 375 Hudson Street,
New York, New York 10014, USA
Penguin Group (Canada), 90 Eglinton Avenue East, Suite 700, Toronto,
Ontario M4P 2Y3, Canada (a division of Pearson Penguin Canada Inc.)
Penguin Books Ltd., 80 Strand, London WC2R 0RL, England
Penguin Ireland, 25 St. Stephen's Green, Dublin 2,
Ireland (a division of Penguin Books Ltd.)
Penguin Group (Australia), 250 Camberwell Road, Camberwell, Victoria 3124,
Australia (a division of Pearson Australia Group Pty. Ltd.)
Penguin Books India Pvt. Ltd., 11 Community Centre, Panchsheel Park,
New Delhi - 110 017, India
Penguin Group (NZ), 67 Apollo Drive, Rosedale, North Shore 0745,
Auckland, New Zealand (a division of Pearson New Zealand Ltd.)
Penguin Books (South Africa) (Pty.) Ltd., 24 Sturdee Avenue,
Rosebank, Johannesburg 2196, South Africa

Penguin Books Ltd., Registered Offices:
80 Strand, London WC2R 0RL, England

First published by Signet, an imprint of New American Library,
a division of Penguin Group (USA) Inc.

First Printing, August 2007
10 9 8 7 6 5 4 3 2 1

This book is dedicated to the pups of Canine Companions for Independence, heroes in the making, and to their puppy raisers, heroes already.

And to my own Destiny, Glitter and Rhythm, and all of the Dixie Dancing Dogs, who bring so much joy to so many every year. May you dance forever!

Chapter One

By the time I was called in, the body had been inside the cabin for at least four days, maybe more. If this had been July instead of October, the odor would have alerted every scavenger in the woods, and probably a few neighbors, long before now. The cool Smoky Mountain nights and moderate daytime temperatures had probably slowed down the decay a good bit. Still, by the looks on the faces of Hanover County's finest when I drove up, what I was about to encounter was not for the faint of heart—or the weak of stomach.

And I'm not even a cop. I'm a dog trainer. Things like this are not exactly in my job description.

The wooded clearing was aglow with late afternoon sunlight. It set the tops of the surrounding trees on fire with bright red and yellow flames and bounced off the hoods and racing blue strip lights of all four Hanover County Sheriff's Department cars, which were edged at every possible angle into the narrow space. The minute I opened the car door I heard the hoarse, frantic, exhausted barking that came from inside the house, and my heart twisted in my chest. I draped a slip-loop leash around my neck and got out of the car.

I singled out the round, middle-aged man standing at the center of a knot of cops and hurried over to him. My uncle Roe had been sheriff of Hanover County for close to thirty years, and today his face showed it. "Hey, Raine," he said, and the cluster of uniforms around him parted. The expressions on the faces of the other officers fell somewhere between relief and regret. They knew, I guess, that when I finished my job, they would have to do theirs. And it would be a very, very unpleasant one.

"Thanks for getting here so quick," Uncle Roe said. He nodded toward the house. "We need to get in there and secure the scene, but we can't get by the dog. Thought you might have a snare or something."

"Shame to shoot him," volunteered Deke, who was not my favorite deputy on the force. "What this county really needs is an animal control officer."

I glared at him. "There's no need to be talking about shooting anything. I can handle this." For reassurance, I shoved my fingers into my jeans pocket and wrapped them around my own weapon—a sandwich bag filled with hot dogs and cheese.

The hoarse, pathetic barking went on and on in the background, muffled by the thick cabin walls and closed windows. How long had he been in there, without food or water, desperately trying to call for help while the person who was responsible for his care lay lifeless and in plain view? The character of the barking sounded hopeless, mindless, a desperate instinct without purpose. It broke my heart.

Uncle Roe started walking with me toward the house, his head down and his fists shoved into the lightweight sheriff's department windbreaker he wore. He moved slowly, in no hurry to reach what lay at the end of the short path.

Guarding the door of the cabin, as though there were anything to be guarded, were two of my favorite members of the force—my almost-ex-husband, Buck, and his female partner, Wyn. Even from a distance I could see that Wyn had the stoic, white-around-the-lips look of a woman who was trying very hard not to be sick, and Buck didn't look much better.

"It looks like suicide," Uncle Roe said. "Gunshot wound between the eyes. A woman; don't have an ID yet. We broke out the back window to get a look inside and make sure the victim was, um, dead." In this part of the country, even supposedly hardened law enforcement officers had the decency to give a respectful pause before consigning a soul to the ever after with the word. He went on, "But the dog is in the front room, between us and the victim, and we can't get in without going past him."

We had reached the front stoop, and Wyn said grimly, "Guess who was the only one small enough to wiggle through the window?"

I grimaced for her. "Was it bad?"

She said simply, "Don't go back there."

Buck gave me a look that was half challenge, half re-proof. "Didn't you bring gloves, or some kind of pole?

Listen to that, Raine. That dog is half crazy. Who knows how long he's been locked up in there, or what he was like before this happened!"

I said firmly, "A pole would only scare him into attack mode. I'll be fine." But I did feel a little foolish for not bringing heavy gloves. Even the best-mannered dog can't be blamed for snapping at a hand when he's terrified. And this dog did not sound as though manners were high on his list of priorities right now.

Uncle Roe said, "Actually it was the dog that alerted the neighbors. A couple who're staying in that cabin across the lake take their morning and evening walks past here every day. After hearing the dog barking like that for four days straight, and trying several times to get someone to come to the door, they called us on an animal neglect complaint."

I swallowed hard. "The dog . . . hasn't been locked in the same room with the body all that time, has it?"

"No," Wyn assured me quickly. "The bedroom door is closed. The dog couldn't get to her."

I released a breath. "Okay, then," I murmured. But I made no move to advance.

Buck said, "We jimmied the lock with a crowbar. But every time we tried to open the door, the dog would charge it."

"He's not charging now," I observed, mostly to myself, and that worried me a little. Ordinarily a dog will rush to the door when a stranger approaches, either to greet or to warn away. From the sound of the barking, I could tell that the dog was somewhere in the center of the room, which meant he was far past the warning stage and would be able to get plenty of speed and power behind the attack when he did decide to charge.

I thrust my hand into my pocket again and brought out a fist filled with cheese and hot dog cubes. "Okay," I said, and moved toward the door.

"Hold on a minute." My uncle withdrew from his pocket a small tin of mentholated salve and snapped off the lid. "Dab a little of this on your upper lip. It cuts the smell."

I had seen big-city cops use this method on TV, but was surprised to see it in real life. "Does this stuff really work?"

"No," said Wyn, looking sick again.

But Uncle Roe took a scoop of the greasy stuff on his fingertip and smeared it beneath my nose. I almost gagged from the strength of the eucalyptus smell, and my eyes watered. I drew in a breath through my mouth and jerked my head toward the yard. "You guys get down off the porch. Don't crowd him."

"No way," said Buck immediately.

"Sorry," agreed Uncle Roe. "You do what you have to do, but we're staying right here."

I hadn't expected anything different. "At least move off to the side. I don't want you scaring him."

Uncle Roe said quietly, "Don't you take any stupid chances, you hear me? I'm not having anybody get hurt here. If that dog goes for you, we're gonna have to shoot him."

I couldn't stare my uncle down like I had Deke, so I didn't even try. Besides, I knew he was right.

I said, "Everybody, just move back. Give me some room."

In the best-case scenario, as far as the police were concerned, the dog would dash through the door the minute I opened it and race off into the woods. That would also be the worst-case scenario as far as the poor dog was concerned, and the last thing that I wanted to happen. So I eased the door open with one shoulder and slipped inside the room sideways, leaving the door open behind me just wide enough to admit daylight. Just so it didn't look like a trap.

The tenor of the barking changed immediately when the door opened, from frantic and crazed to angry and crazed; the sound of a desperate creature who, despite my best efforts, felt trapped. The dark paneled walls reflected little light, and it took my eyes a terrifying moment to adjust to the dimness. In the endless interval until I could see again, I expected to feel sharp teeth piercing some part of my body at any moment.

While my ears were being assaulted with the cacophony of barking and my eyes were struggling to find shapes in the grayness, all the rest of my senses—taste and, yes, touch as well—were inundated by the smell. There was the sharp, unpleasant odor of urine and dog feces, of course; old wood and stale air; not to mention the sickening, now almost sweet aroma of the mentholated balm underneath my nose. But beneath all of that, in fact interwoven with it in a greasy miasma that I could almost see, was a gassy, rotting, sick-sweet odor that I could spend a lifetime trying to describe, and that I will never forget as long as I live.

Think of a raw chicken that has gone bad in the refrigerator. Think of a raccoon that has crawled under the house and died. Put them both together and imagine something ten times worse. I actually gagged on my first breath, and the only thing that kept me from bolting back out through the door was that I got my first glimpse of the dog just then. He was standing in the center of the room with his head down, his ears back and his eyes glinting, barking his furious, terrified, half-growling, half-snapping bark. I would have been a fool to turn my back on him. And I couldn't leave him like that.

A dog's sense of smell is at least five hundred times more acute than ours. And he had been locked up in here with this horror for at least four days. I felt right then as though I wanted to sink to my knees and apologize for the whole human race.

Instead, I lowered my chin and my eyes and turned in perfect profile to him, watching him with my peripheral vision. He was a yellow Lab. I know enough about dogs to realize that a Labrador retriever—the number one dog registered by the AKC for three years running, renowned as the perfect family pet—is just as capable of inflicting severe bite wounds as any rottweiler, Doberman or German shepherd. Their powerful jaws and muscular body type, in fact, would make them particularly suited for attack training—if only they had the aggressive personalities to match.

Everyone loves the Labrador retriever. On big screens and small, from the pages of magazines, newspapers and storybooks, they sit in rowboats and watch the sunset with their beloved masters; they rescue small children from hazardous situations; they fetch beer from the refrigerator on Super Bowl Sunday. They sell cars, houses, insurance and pet food. They are America's dog.

So even though intellectually I knew better, I was relieved that the manic, snarling, jugular-threatening sounds I heard were, in fact, coming from a Labrador retriever. I knew retrievers. This I could handle.

Trying not to make any discernibly sudden movements, I used my thumb to flick one of the hot dog cubes toward him. He didn't notice. I tried again. This one landed close enough to him that he could smell it, and he stopped threatening me long enough to gobble it up. Quickly, before he could recapture the manic barking cycle, I tossed several cubes behind him. He had to turn his back on me to snatch them off the floor. When he looked back at me again I was half a dozen steps closer, though I still maintained my nonthreatening profile and submissive pose. I tossed another treat behind him. He retreated to eat it. I advanced.

By the time I was close enough to stretch out an arm to touch him, I had dropped to a duck-walking crouch, and the life-threatening growls had diminished to an intermittent rumble deep in his chest that was occasionally bracketed by a sound that was somewhere between a groan and a whine. His tail was plastered against his concave belly, his eyes were ravenous and thin streams of drool dripped from both jowls. I opened up my hot dog–filled hand, and he took one cautious step closer, then another. I kept my breathing smooth and even, and

I did not look at him. His hunger overcame his fear and he gobbled up the remaining treats in my hand. I turned and in a single smooth motion whipped the leash from around my neck over his head, tightening the loop around his neck.

This was the most dangerous part of the operation. I was close enough and he was fast enough that he could have easily taken a hunk out of my face or my hand if he had been so inclined. At the very least he could have gone into a wild bucking fit in which one of us was sure to be hurt. He did neither of those things.

The minute he felt the loop on his neck he looked at me, and if a dog can be said to experience emotion, I would swear the emotion that swept through his eyes was relief. This was a dog who knew what a leash was for and who associated it with good things. This surprised me, because he was not wearing a collar.

There are many good reasons for a person to leave a dog uncollared, of course—an allergy or coat breakage, a recent bath in which the collar was removed and forgotten, or the fact that the dog is minutes away from entering the conformation or agility ring. Obviously the last two instances did not apply to this dog, but I confess I am overall a little judgmental on the subject of collars. In the area in which I live, a dog without a collar usually means an owner who doesn't have sense enough to take care of his pet.

I offered my open hand to the yellow Lab and he snuffled and licked it, searching for more hot dogs. I quickly dug out more treats and let him scarf them up while I gently stroked his ears and murmured to him reassuringly.

From outside Buck called, "Raine, you okay?"

I didn't answer because I didn't want to startle the dog. Instead I murmured, "Okay, big fellow, let's see about finding you a real meal, hmm?"

I stood up slowly, holding a cube of cheese in front of the dog's nose to lead him toward the door. But instead of following complacently, like the good dog he had proven himself to be at heart, he suddenly turned and bolted toward the back of the house, pulling me with such force that he almost jerked me off my feet. I gave an involuntary cry —"Hey!"—which caused Buck, Roe and Wyn to come rushing through the front door with their hands on their sidearms.

I concentrated on holding on to the leash as the big Lab flung himself on the closed door of what I instinctively knew to be the bedroom. There were claw marks on the door frame and in the finish of the pine-paneled door, where he had alternately tried to dig and push his way inside to find his mistress. Now he was trying, in the best dog language he knew, to get me to open the door.

Uncle Roe demanded behind me, "You okay? Got him under control?"

"Yeah, everything's fine." I didn't turn around, but slipped one arm around the dog's shoulders while tugging gently on the leash, dislodging his paws from the door. "Come on, sweetie, let's go."

The dog gave a plaintive whine and dropped to all fours, responding reluctantly to my leash tugs as we

moved away from the door and the awful truth that lay
behind it.

Uncle Roe said, "Thanks, hon. Get on outside now."

"I'm going to take the dog to the vet and have him
checked out, okay?"

"Try not to touch anything on your way out."

He was pulling on a pair of gloves, his face filled with
reluctance for what he was about to do. Buck and Wyn
gave me wide berth as I moved the dog past them, which
was not really necessary. The Lab could not stop looking
over his shoulder and was far more worried about
whether to follow my lead on the leash or to try to make
another run for the door than with defending himself
against strangers.

For myself, I was more than anxious to be out of the
cabin before the bedroom door was opened. The truth is,
I have seen dead bodies before. But they are not something that I go out of my way to encounter.

In addition to my mostly full-time dog training and
boarding business, I do seasonal part-time work for the
forest service and am always on call, with my golden retriever, Cisco, for search and rescue work. Our little
community is only a few miles away from the Appalachian Trail, in the heart of the Smoky Mountain
wilderness, and most of the time the hikers, campers and
lost tourists we are called to search for are found scared
and hungry, but otherwise fine. Occasionally they are
not. Those times when a rescue operation turns into a recovery mission are not the kind of thing you want to
think about before going to bed at night. And you never,

ever want to repeat the experience if you can possibly help it.

I did not intend to linger. The last thing I wanted to do was to look back inside that door when Uncle Roe opened it. But, of course, the dog saw Uncle Roe cautiously push the door open. He lunged for it. I lunged for him. And what I saw, even though it was barely a glimpse, would remain frozen in my mind forever. Not because it was so horrific, but because it was so sad.

My view was of one corner of the room. Broken glass on the floor from the window Wyn had broken. A log-frame bed covered with a polka-dotted quilt. Beside it one of those laurel-wood chairs that are so popular for their rustic appeal, but impossibly uncomfortable to sit in. Someone had chosen to sit in it, though. And she had never gotten up.

A bloated arm covered in chambray hung over the side of the chair, fingers just visible. Beneath those fingers on the floor lay a large-caliber pistol, the kind that could literally blow a person's brains out if fired at close range. And that, I realized as I looked again at the quilt, was exactly what it had done.

I closed my fingers around the scruff of the dog's neck and pulled him with me as I staggered, senses reeling, toward the front door. He followed without protest, as though he had been rendered as helpless as I had been by the sight.

I made my away across the small yard to my SUV, oblivious to the uniformed officers and the looks they gave me, oblivious to the flurry of activity as Buck stood on the front porch and began to relay orders, oblivious to

the flashing lights and crackling radios and to everything, in fact, except the now-complacent, brokenhearted
creature on the other end of the leash. I opened the back
of the SUV, where I kept a wire dog crate in order to
safely transport my own and other people's dogs when I
had to. When I opened the door of the crate, the yellow
Lab jumped in, just as though he had been doing it all his
life.

At the time, I barely noticed.

I secured the crate, closed the door of the SUV and
got behind the driver's seat. I even turned on the engine
and adjusted the vents so that the dog would have plenty
of fresh air. And then I just folded my arms over the top
of the steering wheel and sat there, trying to breathe
deeply. It was a long time before I felt steady enough to
drive.

Chapter Two

My name is Raine Stockton, and I have been around law enforcement all my life. Most people still think of me as "Judge Stockton's daughter," since my father was a district court judge here in Hanover County for the last thirty years of his life. My mother's brother, Uncle Roe, has been unopposed for the post of sheriff since he first took office back in the seventies, and everyone seems to like it that way. I married Deputy Buck Lawson not once but twice, and though we currently live apart—and I keep my maiden name—we still can't quite make up our minds whether we are better off with or without each other. When I put on my forest service uniform, people often call me "Officer," and I don't always correct them. I have a deep and natural respect for the work that law officers do. And after what I had witnessed today, I was more convinced than ever than I wanted no part of it.

Which is why, I suppose, I found the persistent questions of people who always assume I know more about police matters than I actually do more annoying today than usual.

To be fair, it was not Ken Withers, our local vet, who bombarded me with questions, although he was the one who probably had the most right to do so. After all, I had burst into his office without an appointment or even a phone call, dragging a strange dog and blurting out an even stranger story about his having been locked inside a cabin for days with a dead body. Doc Withers, in fact, didn't even raise an eyebrow. He was what you might call a man of few words, who preferred to gather his information through the tools of his trade: the stethoscope, the microscope, his own expert touch and powers of observation.

His wife, Ethel, ran the front office and acted as assistant when necessary, and their daughter, Crystal, now a senior in high school, acted as vet tech on the afternoons and weekends. It was they who, big eyed with shock and curiosity, couldn't ask me questions fast enough.

"Good Lord," exclaimed Ethel, coming quickly from behind the reception desk. She was a rather large woman with a fondness for flowered work smocks and gray pin curls, which bobbed when she was excited. The curls were bobbing now. "Who was she? Anyone we know?"

I shook my head, following the Labrador as Doc Withers calmly took his leash and led him into the examining room. "I don't think they have an ID yet."

"Whose cabin was it?" Crystal wanted to know, bringing up the rear of the procession that crowded into the small examining room. "I bet it was some of those people from the coast. I heard they have some wild parties up there at the lake, lots of drugs."

Her mother looked at her sharply. "Where would you hear a thing like that?"

Crystal shrugged a typical teenager's shrug.

Ethel said, "Was it a gun, did you say? I heard on one of those TV shows that women don't use guns to kill themselves. Too messy."

I thought that was the most ridiculous thing I'd ever heard. If you were going to kill yourself, male or female, the last thing you'd worry about was the mess you'd leave behind. After all, if one thing was certain, it was that you wouldn't be the one who had to clean it up.

But I said, "This one did." Then I hurried quickly to help Doc Withers lift the quivering dog onto the table. "I don't think he's hurt," I said, "just scared and starving. I wanted you to check him out, though."

"Shots?"

"I don't know," I admitted. "He seems kind of well mannered. He might have been pretty well taken care of. But there's no way of knowing."

He grunted. I knew he would innoculate the dog, with no charge to me, against all contagious diseases before he released him to come home to my dogs. And he would never say a word about the cost. He was just that way.

Ethel insisted, "Maybe it wasn't suicide at all. Do you think it was? Is that what the sheriff thinks? Are they calling in the state boys?"

Way too much television, I thought. I said anxiously to

her husband, "He probably hasn't had anything to drink in three or four days either."

Doc Withers pinched a fold of the dog's skin between his fingers and grunted. Even I could see that the lack of elasticity indicated definite dehydration. He peeled back the dog's lips and checked his gums.

Crystal said, "Was Deputy Lawson there? I bet he was. I bet he was on the job, in charge of everything."

Crystal, like most other females who had ever encountered him, had a shameless crush on my husband. Frankly, I don't understand it. Buck is cute enough: tall, well built, gorgeous hair. But he's no Brad Pitt. Maybe it's the uniform.

In my younger days, I used to get furious with Buck for his unaccountable appeal to the opposite sex, as though he was deliberately putting out a sex pheromone designed to attract other women. Now I barely noticed— except when he acted on it, which, unfortunately, was far too often for a so-called married man. And that, in a nutshell, was why we no longer lived together as husband and wife.

Ethel said, "When do you think they'll have an ID? Are they collecting DNA evidence?"

Her husband, meantime, was running a microchip scanner over the dog. I took his grunt to mean a negative finding.

More and more pet owners these days are having their vets implant microchips in their dogs with their personal information and a link to a lost-and-found service, in case of emergencies just like this. When a dog runs away during a thunderstorm, gets lost on vacation, is separated from its owner during a car accident, house fire, or natural disaster like Hurricane Katrina—there is absolutely, hands down, no better chance of recovering a lost pet than a microchip. Almost all veterinarians, animal shelters and rescue groups routinely scan every new dog they see for the presence of an identifying chip.

With the lack of a microchip, I lost my best hope of identifying the woman who by now was probably being zipped into a body bag and transported via slow-moving ambulance to Sutter's Funeral Home, official headquarters of our county coroner.

Crystal said, "I bet they call out the whole force for a thing like this. Do you think they'll do a roadblock?"

Said her father, "Like to keep him overnight, give him some IV fluids. Should be fine."

"Thank you." My gratitude was heartfelt. "I'll pick him up first thing in the morning."

Crystal said, "Do you want us to give him a bath? He kind of, well, you know—smells."

I turned to her and I smiled. "Crystal," I said, "that would be wonderful."

I, on the other hand, knew I could stand under the shower for days but would never get the smell of that cabin out of my hair.

"I'll be back for you, big guy," I promised as I left the examining room. "You're going to be fine."

"Wait." Ethel focused on her job as I reached the reception room. "We need to make a file. Do you have a name?"

I stared at her blankly. "What?"

"For the dog," she explained with an exaggerated

show of patience. "We need a name for the dog. For the file."

I glanced back toward the exam room, where the quivering mass of yellow Labrador was still huddled on the table. I started to tell her that, in the absence of psychic powers, I had no earthly way of knowing the dog's name, and that, given the fact that I had just spent twenty minutes rescuing him from the kind of hell no dog—much less a human—should ever have to set foot in, I thought my good deeds for the day were up to quota. She could think of a name.

But then I remembered the dog barking himself hoarse, day and night, until someone finally noticed. I remembered the claw marks on the door. I remembered how, even when he finally had his chance to be free, he had run back to find his mistress. And I remembered the alertness in his eyes when I called him a hero. I said quietly, "Yeah. I've got a name."

I looked back at her. "Hero," I said. "His name is Hero."

The story has it that my early ancestors, refugees from Scotland after that unfortunate business with Bonnie Prince Charlie, settled deep in the hills of North Carolina and began to build a life for themselves. They befriended the Cherokee, remained neutral during the War for Independence, and kept out of sight when the Blue Coats and the Gray Coats started squabbling. This was a pretty common story for those who chose to make their lives in what we like to think of as God's vest pocket. This close to paradise, why would anyone want more? And when you've already got pretty much everything a person could ask for, what's the point in fighting? Peace-loving became something of a habit over the years, and so did staying put and minding your own business.

Sometime after the Civil War, an English school-teacher by the name of Elias Stockton came along and married the prettiest girl on the ridge, or so my grand-mother used to tell it. He built her a fine painted house on a gently sloping knoll at the foot of Hawk Mountain with tall glass windows that came all the way from Charleston. I've often wondered how he afforded such luxury on a schoolteacher's salary. Trust fund? Or moonshine?

But it was a fine house, with impressive white columns, heart pine floors and sturdy outbuildings constructed of native chestnut. For generations it was both a landmark and a status symbol, until the county road was built in 1956 and travelers no longer had to pass the "big white house with the columns" on their way to just about everywhere. What must have seemed a blow to the pride of Grandma and Grandpa Stockton turned out to be a boon for everyone who lived in the house after them, though. What had once been a well-traveled dirt road is now a private drive leading straight to the house, and today you can sit on the front porch and see nothing but rolling mountains, hear nothing but birds.

Well, sometimes you hear a few barking dogs.

The house was so finely built that it has survived almost 150 years of children, marital disputes, taxes and natural and man-made disasters—and so have most of the outbuildings. A fellow stopped by some years ago and offered me enough per linear foot for the boards of my barn that I could have built an entirely new house on the profit. The only catch was that I would have had to tear down the barn. I decided instead to turn it into a dog kennel.

It was not that training and boarding dogs was my first choice of career. When I graduated from the University of North Carolina with a wildlife services degree, my options were wide open. What I chose to do was to marry Buck Lawson and to stay right here in Hanover County. The first choice I regretted almost immediately; the second, never.

When the funding for my "real" job with the Department of the Environment and Natural Resources ran out, I was left with three assets: a little bit of talent for training dogs, an even smaller amount of cash and one incredible golden retriever named Cassidy. Cassidy and I had made something of a name for ourselves as a search and rescue team while working for the DNR and had gone on to win awards in popular dog sports and therapy dog pursuits. She not only taught me everything I know about dogs; she taught me most of what I know about life. Sharing some of the knowledge with other people seemed like a logical next step.

My part-time work for the forest service is mostly during the peak tourist seasons of the summer and fall, and without Dog Daze Boarding and Training Center we'd all get pretty hungry waiting for summer to roll around. By "we" I mean me and the four dogs who now share the big white-columned house with me, leave claw marks on the heart pine floors and nose smudges on the Charleston windows and lounge shamelessly on my mother's brocade sofa when they think I'm not looking.

Unfortunately, Cassidy is no longer among the canine residents of the house, but is enjoying what I believe to be the abundance of the eternal reward reserved for dogs of her caliber. The golden retriever who came barreling out of the dog door and into the fenced back enclosure to greet me as I pulled into the circular drive was Cassidy's spitting image, though—as well he should be, since Cisco was her grandson. He flung himself onto the black chain-link in an ecstacy of welcome, barking the story of his day and clawing the wire to hurry my exit from the car. When I didn't open the door fast enough to suit him, he threw himself to the ground, rolled over twice, jumped up and took a lightning lap around the yard, then hurled himself onto the fence again, clenching a rubber bone between his teeth as though trying to bribe me with his cuteness. I couldn't help smiling. That's the thing about golden retrievers: No matter how rotten your day, they can always find a way to make you smile.

I said, "Cisco, down," as I got out of the car. Obediently, my big golden boy dropped to his belly, tail swishing in the dried leaves, still grinning around a mouthful of rubber bone. I unlocked the gate and stepped inside, closed the gate securely behind me, then held my arms open wide, "Okay, good boy!"

Cisco sailed through the air and threw himself into my arms. I staggered under the weight of the eighty-pound dog, whom I could hold for only a few seconds, but we had played this game many times before. I hugged him tight, he slid to the ground and we enjoyed a quick game of tug with the rubber bone before I asked him to drop it. He surrendered his prize to me, I praised him to the skies and then I quickly returned the toy to him.

But this time Cisco was far more interested in sniffing every inch of my jeans and my shoes than he was in racing triumphantly around the yard with the bone, as was his usual custom. They say a dog can gather more information with his nose than a human can with all five senses put together, and I had lived with dogs long enough to believe it. I winced a little as I imagined the picture Cisco was putting together from the traces of scent on my clothes.

I ruffled his fur. "Come on, fellow, let's go eat."

The word "eat" is high priority in the canine vocabulary and will almost always take precedence over any other activity on the agenda. Cisco's ears perked up, he stopped his sniffing and he raced me to the door.

Unfortunately for him, the phone started ringing almost before I'd closed the door behind me, and dinner was postponed. I snatched up the portable as I moved toward the living room, where the other three dogs waited patiently in their crates.

"Is everything all right?" Maude wanted to know.

Maude Braselton is my partner in Dog Daze, the smartest trainer I have ever known, and probably my best friend in the world. She is a slim, athletic sixty with short iron gray hair and a crisp British accent. She had run my father's office, and later his courtroom, for more than thirty-five years with the same brisk efficiency with which she managed her kennel of award-winning golden retrievers, and I couldn't remember a time she hadn't been part of the family. When I had rushed out of the kennel in the middle of a training session this afternoon, all I had told her was that there was an emergency. In truth, I hadn't known much more than that myself. Naturally she was worried.

"It was awful," I told her, leaning over to unlatch the crate door of Majesty, the collie. "Some woman—a tourist—committed suicide in one of the cabins up on Wild Turkey Lane. Her dog had been locked inside for days."

"Good Lord," said Maude, managing to convey in those two words all the horror, disgust and pathos the actual scene had inspired. And then she added, because she knew what was important, "What kind of dog?"

"Yellow Lab. I took him to Doc Withers. He was dehydrated and traumatized, of course, but otherwise seemed okay."

"How unspeakably horrid."

I said, "Yeah."

Majesty, having finished her leisurely stretch, shook out her magnificent sable coat and began the business of thoroughly inspecting my jeans and shoes with her nose, just as Cisco had done. I shuffled over to the other two crates, trying not to trip over her.

"Was she alone?" Maude asked.

"The woman? She seemed to be. Can you imagine how terrible her life must have been for her to plan a trip to the mountains—in the fall, when everything is so beautiful—and then rent a cabin just to kill herself?"

"No," replied Maude sensibly, "I can't. What makes you think she came here just to kill herself? Maybe whatever happened to push her over the edge occurred after she got here."

I considered that as I undid the rope tie that held the slide bolt closed on Mischief's crate. Mischief was an Australian shepherd with far too much manual dexterity for her own good, and I had to tie her crate door closed or she would open the lock by herself. Her sister, Magic, was just as clever, but fortunately not as adventurous. I opened both crate doors, and twin blurs of Australian shepherd energy streaked past me, skidded on a turn and then raced back to join Majesty in the sniff-fest of my feet and ankles. Cisco, tail waving, pushed himself into the fray.

I said, "I don't know. I got the impression she hadn't been there long enough for anything to happen. They hadn't found any ID when I left."

"Which cabin was it?"

"The first one, as you come around the bend of the lake, across from Deadman's Cove."

"Not Letty Cranston's place?"

"You know who owns it?"

"She used to be in my bridge club before her husband died and she moved to Hilton Head full-time. He had more money than God, left her several properties—a ranch in Montana, a beach house in Florida, a place on Pawleys Island . . . I didn't know she was renting out the cabin, though."

"I don't think Uncle Roe knew who owned it."

"I'm sure he does by now, dear."

"Do you know how to get in touch with her? Just in case they can't identify the victim."

"I'll see if I can find a number."

I gave up trying to escape the dogs and sat down in the middle of the floor, letting them snuffle and crawl over me to their hearts' content. I had seen too much of the bad side of life today—even the bad side of life for a dog—and I was not inclined to push away anything that was warm and affectionate.

"What about the Lab? He wasn't wearing any ID, I suppose."

"Not even a collar. The funny thing is, though, he seemed like a well-trained dog. He responded to the leash and jumped right into the crate when I opened the car door. I can't help wondering—"

But I never finished the sentence. A gunshot exploded out of nowhere, and I dropped the phone, covered my head and screamed.

Chapter Three

Three more rifle shots exploded—*Pow! Pow! Pow!*—and the dogs burst into hysterics, racing toward the door and barking a cacophony of wild objection. I shouted, "Damn it!" and snatched up the phone.

"Sorry!" I said, raising my voice to be heard over the dogs. "But did you *hear* that? It was practically in my living room! I swear to God if I ever find out who's hunting this close to private property I'll have a piece of their hide!" I covered the mouthpiece of the telephone and shouted, "Dogs! Quiet!"

Three of the dogs trotted obediently back to me. Majesty, whose job it was to keep the property and all its occupants safe from invasion, set forth two more indignant barks—the canine equivalent of "and don't come back!"—before returning to me for petting.

"They are getting awfully close to the house," agreed Maude worriedly. "The kennel has been in an uproar all week. Didn't you post NO HUNTING signs?"

"Every ten feet all along the property line," I fumed.

"We're obviously dealing with a bunch of cross-eyed cretins who either can't read the English language or are too drunk to see. Lucky for them I happen to know the sheriff's department has its hands full this afternoon or I'd have the law out here so fast—"

"I think," suggested Maude gently, "you may be a little jumpy."

I sighed, knowing that at least part of my outrage was sheer embarrassment for having screamed and dropped the phone at the sound of a rifle shot. It was autumn, and men with rifles stalking the woods were a fact of life. It wasn't as though I didn't know that. "I think I have right to be," I said, "after what I saw this afternoon."

"Agreed."

"And they *are* too close to the house."

"Absolutely agreed. Why don't you call Reese Pickens and complain?"

"He doesn't own that land anymore. You know that."

"Dollars to donuts he knows exactly who's hunting there, though."

"Maybe," I agreed reluctantly. "One thing I've got to say for the Pickens boys, the *only* thing," I interjected, "is that in all the years they hunted Hawk Mountain they never once fired a shot toward this house."

"That's because your daddy would have skinned them alive and hung them up by their privates if they had."

"And because mountain folk, even if they are as mean as snakes, know the rules of hunting. It's these damn city idiots—"

"Raine," said Maude, "go feed the dogs. Have a bath.

Make yourself a nice supper and get a good night's sleep. You'll feel better in the morning."

Since Reese Pickens had sold Hawk Mountain to an Atlanta developer last spring, Maude had heard my bitter observations about damn-fool big-city jackasses more than once, and so had everyone else who would stand still long enough to listen. And I knew that today my irritation, however justified, had its roots in a much darker problem—the smell of death that I couldn't get out of my nostrils, the sight of the bloated arm and the gun lying on the floor beneath it.

Subdued, I said, "Yeah, I guess so. Let me know if you track down Mrs. Cranston."

"I'm sure the police will reach her long before I do. Good night, dear."

The sunset was putting on a magnificent display over the red and gold mountaintops that were visible from the kitchen window as I quickly filled each of four dishes and served them to my canine companions. Dogs are wonderfully single-minded and completely accepting of whatever the moment has to offer, so by the time the first scoop came out of the kibble bin they had completely forgotten about the bizarre smells on my clothing and the gunfire and were focused on only one thing: dinner. I, however, could not get the smell out of my mind, off my clothes, out of my hair. All I wanted was a shower.

But first I had to feed our boarders—the kennel was full this time of year—and turn them all out for one last romp. By the time I had scooped all the poop, settled everyone inside with a good-night dog biscuit, and locked the kennel building, it was practically dark and noticeably colder. I hurried upstairs and into the long-awaited shower.

I stayed there until the hot water ran out, lathering and relathering my hair, scrubbing my skin until it was pink with a syrupy sweet purple body wash that someone had given me for Christmas. And it was while I was standing there, letting the last of the hot water sluice away the soapsuds, that I remembered something odd.

I hadn't seen a dog dish in the cabin. The front room was open to the kitchen, and there had been no sign of a dog dish in either room. I travel with my dogs a great deal, to shows, on search and rescue missions, to training workshops and conferences, and whether I am setting up camp in a tent city or checking into a dog-friendly motel, the first thing I do—before I unpack my suitcases or check the schedule—is to fill a bowl with water and set it on the floor for my dog. Doesn't everyone?

I tried to imagine the kinds of things that would keep me from looking after the welfare of my dog first and couldn't think of a single one. Not even contemplated suicide.

But that was just me.

I slipped into a cozy pair of flannel pajamas with golden retrievers printed on them and went into the bedroom, toweling my hair. There I stopped still, hands on my hips, and glared. "Get your mangy carcass off my bed," I ordered.

Cisco was stretched out atop my bed, all four paws in the air, an expression of absolute bliss on his face as he gave over to having his belly rubbed by my almost-ex-husband.

Buck, resting his head on his propped-up arm while he stroked Cisco's silky white underside with the other hand, glanced up. "Cisco resents that."

"I was talking about you." I walked forward and snapped him lightly with the towel. "Off, both of you. I hate dog hair on my bed, and you're teaching him to disobey me."

Cisco rolled over genially and hopped off the bed, grinning as he shook out his coat. To a dog, a moment stolen is a moment earned, and no amount of scolding would have spoiled his pleasure. Of course it would have been pointless to scold him once he was *off* the bed, so I scolded Buck instead.

"What are you doing here, anyway? You just walk in and make yourself at home now?"

I should point out that Buck and I are at a rather awkward point in our on-again, off-again relationship: not quite on, but very far from off. In other words, he was not entirely as much of a stranger as he once had been to the bed where he now lounged so comfortably. And while I managed to keep up a pretty good scowl, my tone was not very convincing.

He propped himself up into a sitting position against the pillows and extended a hand to me. "Just wanted to see how you were holding up."

I let him pull me down beside him and settled into the curve of his arm. "Not so bad. Okay, I guess. I can still smell it."

His face brushed my damp curls. "I smell lilacs."

He had showered and changed into jeans and a soft, much-washed sweater. He smelled like soap.

I said, "The vet thinks the dog is going to be okay, just dehydrated. No microchip. Did you find out who she was?"

"Not a clue. The house was completely empty."

I twisted around to look at him. "What do you mean, empty? Not even her purse?"

"Sweetheart," he told me, "not even a car."

I stared at him. "Then how did she get there?"

He lifted a shoulder. "It's what's you might call a mystery."

"I mean, it's not like you could just hike in off that highway to that cabin, and even if you did you'd have *something* . . . a backpack, a wallet . . ."

"Apparently all she had was a gun."

"And a dog," I reminded him. I settled back against his shoulder, frowning. "It doesn't make sense."

"I always did say you had the mind of a lawman."

"Not even a bag of dog food?"

"Not even."

"And it was definitely suicide?"

"It was definitely a gunshot wound through the center of the head, and there's no evidence to indicate it wasn't suicide."

"At least she locked the dog out."

"What?"

"Before she . . . you know." I shrugged uncomfortably and let my hand drop over the side of the bed to fondle Cisco's silky ear. "She closed the door so he wouldn't see it."

Buck was silent, and both of us pondered, for a moment, our own separate gruesome thoughts.

Then I said, "Maude says she knows who owns the cabin."

"Letty Cranston, we know. We've left messages at each of her three houses."

"Maybe she didn't rent the cabin. Maybe this woman, whoever she was, found the cabin empty and decided to take advantage of it. She might even have found the gun there."

"Maybe. We're checking the registration."

"It's just weird. Where's her car? Did the neighbors see anything?"

"There's only that one other couple on the lake, the ones who heard the dog barking. They say they never noticed a car. Of course, it's pretty isolated up there. If they hadn't been in the habit of taking daily walks, they never would have known anybody else was on the lake."

"Weird," I repeated.

He tilted his head down at me. "Did you eat?"

"No. Did you bring anything?"

"No. Do you want to go out?"

"No."

"Do you have any eggs?"

"Will you make French toast?"

He kissed my curls lightly as he got up. "Supper will be served in fifteen minutes. Dry your hair before you catch cold. The temperature is really dropping out there. The radio says frost."

I couldn't help smiling as I watched him go, Cisco

bouncing down the stairs after him. Sometimes he was really nice to have around.

I don't think I've ever met anyone who is as comfortable in his own skin as is Buck Lawson. He knows exactly who he is and what his place in the world is, and he never questions or complains about either. He has that kind of easy self-assurance that women of all ages find incredibly attractive, and I admit, I'm one of them. He stole my heart when I was fifteen and I've never really gotten it back, not completely.

I'm not saying this is a good thing. It simply is.

When I came down in the morning a little after six, he had already taken Cisco for a run, brought in a load of firewood, fed the dogs and made coffee. He didn't do any of these things to score points or earn my gratitude, but simply because they needed to be done.

Buck placed a cup of coffee into my groping hands as I slid into a chair at the kitchen table, yawning. The two Australian shepherds nuzzled me excitedly, wiggling their tailless butts and trying to convince me they hadn't already eaten. Majesty, the collie, looked up from her worn blue flannel bed by the wood-burning stove and woofed a soft greeting. Flames glowed amber behind the glass doors of the stove, and the kitchen felt cozy.

"You'd better get a move on if you expect to make the nine o'clock service," Buck said, wiping the counter of toast crumbs. Cisco sat worshipfully at his feet, eyes fixed on the countertop in hopeful anticipation that a crumb or two might fall his way.

I stared at him. "Oh, crap," I said. "It's Sunday."

"God'll get you for that."

"What I mean is I told Doc Withers I'd pick up the dog today, but the office will be closed." I hurried to the telephone that sat on the edge of the kitchen counter. "I hate for the poor guy to stay another night at the vet's."

Buck stopped me as I reached for the phone. "Don't be calling the man at six o'clock in the morning on a Sunday. It can wait until this afternoon."

I had to agree: six a.m. was an inconsiderate hour at which to make a call, especially when dealing with a doctor or a vet, who might well have been up all night anyway. "Maybe I can pick him up after church," I said, returning the receiver to its stand. "I'll give them a call after I get the kennel dogs fed." I took a quick gulp of coffee. "Did everyone in here eat?"

"Yeah, and don't let them tell you otherwise." He clasped the back of my neck briefly with a warm hand and brushed a kiss across my nose. "I've got to get home and change. See you later."

"At church?"

"Can't. I'm on duty."

"I'm going to Aunt Mart's for dinner. I'll bring home some leftovers if you want to stop by later."

"Sounds like an offer I can't refuse." He lingered, hands lightly clasping my shoulders, a rueful smile in his eyes. "This is a little crazy, you know."

I slid my gaze away uncomfortably.

"I'm here more than I'm at home. My house is starting to feel like a big closet."

I said, "Maybe we're spending too much time together."

"Maybe we're not spending enough."

"It's not even light outside," I said. "I haven't had my first cup of coffee. This is not a good time to have this conversation."

I couldn't help noticing that his eyes were no longer smiling. "Soon, okay?"

I nodded because, really, what else could I do?

I walked him to the door, cradling my coffee. "Oh," I said, suddenly remembering. "Did Dolly Amstead call you?"

"From the bank?" He looked surprised. "About what?"

"About helping to set up the Pet Fair booth at the Fall Festival next weekend. We need your truck to transport some of the agility equipment and a strong pair of arms to set up the puppy playground."

"Why didn't you just ask me?"

I smiled sweetly. "Because I am not in charge."

"Ah," he said, nodding. We both knew Dolly had control issues. "Well, tell her she'd better not waste any time getting in touch with me. My social calendar fills up pretty quickly these days. Who knows when I might get a better offer?"

I slid an arm around his waist, holding the coffee cup out to the side as I tilted my face up to his. "Does it, now? You got a girlfriend or something?"

He accepted my invitation for a kiss, and when I opened my eyes, his were once again smiling. "Or something." He touched my chin with an index finger. "Save me some leftovers."

He opened the door on the cold dark morning, and I

shivered and closed it behind him again quickly. In another moment headlights flashed on the windowpane, and I could hear the muffled barking of every dog in the kennel. I sighed and finished my coffee quickly. My day had begun.

In small communities like mine, going to church is more than a matter of religious expression; it's also something of a cross between a town hall meeting and a block party, a chance to mingle with your neighbors and catch up on the goings-on. We sing a little "Abide with Me," listen to a sermon on how to be better neighbors and spend the rest of the time finding out who's in the hospital, who has a new baby, what time the spaghetti supper for the volunteer fire department starts and so on. Dolly Amstead got up and made a lengthy announcement about the Pet Fair that would be held in conjunction with this year's Hansonville Fall Festival in order to raise money for a badly needed animal shelter, and directed people to get in touch with me if they wanted to volunteer to help with the booth, buy tickets for any of the events or sign up for the pet parade. I waggled my fingers from the middle pew where I sat with Aunt Mart and Uncle Roe when heads turned to find me. You really do have to admire Dolly's managerial style: She has a wonderful way of delegating all the work while still managing to hold on to both the control *and* the credit.

I had managed to catch Ethel Withers at home just before I left for church. She told me that the dog I had decided to call Hero was off the IV and was on a bland diet of chicken broth and rice. They were on their way to

Hickory to spend the day with her mother, but if I wanted to pick the dog up after church she would leave him in the back kennel run. I thanked her and promised to pick him up in a couple of hours.

I knew that Hero was perfectly safe in the shady kennel run at the veterinary hospital. There was a padlock on the gate to which I had been given the combination; the nine-foot-tall run was curved inward to discourage jumping or climbing escapees; he had plenty of water and shelter in case of rain, of which there was not the slightest sign. Nonetheless I was anxious about leaving him there unsupervised.

I gave my Aunt Mart's plump shoulders a quick hug as soon as the benediction was pronounced. "I'll be over as soon as I get the dog settled in at home," I promised. I had explained to both my aunt and Uncle Roe about the situation with the dog as soon as I had seen them that morning. "It shouldn't take me more than an hour."

"Oh, honey, there's no point in you driving from one end of the county to the other. Bring the dog over to our place with you. He'll be okay for a few hours while we visit."

"Are you sure?" Despite my aunt's unabashed adoration of Majesty, my pretty collie, she was not exactly a dog person, and her knickknack-filled house and immaculate lawn were definitely not dog friendly.

"We can put him in the barn," she assured me.

I smiled. "That's okay. I've got a crate in the truck, and I can leave the back open. As long as he doesn't bark."

"What's a little barking? He'll be fine. You run on, now."

Uncle Roe, who was, after all, a politician, was busy shaking hands and chatting with his neighbors, so I just waved to him in passing as I squeezed through the crowd. I left a stack of fliers about the Pet Fair on the vestibule table next to a sign-up list for Meals on Wheels drivers and some brochures about an after-school Bible study program. Out of the corner of my eye I saw Dolly waving to catch my attention from the back of the crowd, but I managed to slide out into the crisp autumn sunshine before she could catch me. There I found myself face to face with Reese Pickens.

When talking about our little corner of the mountains to outsiders, residents will often conclude with, "And ninety-nine percent of the people who live here are good, decent, hardworking folks." In the back of most people's minds when they think about the one percent would be someone named Pickens.

Earlier in the year, Reese's son, Luke—known for his violent temper and flagrant drug and alcohol abuse—had been murdered and dumped on the side of the road. Some people thought Reese himself might have had a hand in that, and I was one of them. But my dispute with Reese went deeper than that. In March, he had sold Hawk Mountain, whose shadow had sheltered my family home for generations, to a developer with some outrageous idea of turning it into a fly-in resort for the super-rich. What once had been one of the most serene vistas in the county was now crisscrossed with the ugly scar of access roads and utility right-of-ways, the wildlife which had once called the mountain home had been displaced—mostly into people's backyards—and I was slowly being forced to face the fact that the only life I had ever known here in Hanover County was about to undergo some major changes.

My inclination was to walk past him without speaking, but as luck would have it, we were standing only a few feet away from the preacher, who was greeting parishioners as they left the church full of compliments on the timeliness of his message about loving thy neighbor. So I said, as politely as I could, "Good morning, Mr. Pickens."

He was a big, silver-haired man with a penchant for expensive Stetson hats. He tipped his hat to me now— this one with a sterling eagle's head at the crown—and replied, "Miss Raine. How's every little thing going over at your place?"

I regarded him cooly. "Well enough. You wouldn't happen to know who's been hunting over on Hawk Mountain the past few days, would you?"

"That's private property," he reminded me, and he looked far too pleased with himself to suit me. "How do you figure I'd know what's going on out there?"

"They're getting awfully close to the *edge* of private property," I told him, unsmiling. "And unless they want to wind up on the wrong side of the law, somebody ought to remind them about a few of the rules of gun safety."

He chuckled. "Miss Raine, you are a sight. Always huffing and puffing about rules and regulations and what's right and what's wrong. One of these days you're going to finally kick that deputy lawman of yours to the curb, and your uncle's going to retire and nobody's going to give a fancy rat's behind who your daddy used to be. Who's going to stop and listen to what you've got to say then, huh?"

I refused to let him goad me. "How's Cindy doing these days?"

Cindy Winston and her daughter, Angel—or I should say, *their* daughter, since Reese was, according to Cindy, the child's father—had both been part of the tangled scandal that surrounded Luke Pickens's death in the spring. It was not a pretty story, and it still bothered me that Reese Pickens should have any sort of guardianship over the little girl, Angel, even if it did mean that she would be financially secure for the rest of her life.

He said, without change of expression, "Why, I can't say I rightly know. Last I heard, she up and moved to Fort Lauderdale."

I had heard that too. I had just wanted to see his expression when I asked. I said, "I'm not a bit surprised."

I turned to the preacher and extended my hand, "Enjoyed the sermon, Pastor," and Reese Pickens moved on.

True to her word, Crystal had bathed the yellow Lab, who was waiting for me in the back kennel run of the veterinary hospital. He smelled like vanilla and looked slightly less emaciated than he had the day before, but he did not even raise his head from the sun-dappled concrete pad on which he lay when I approached the gate. He made no sign of protest when I slipped the leash around his neck, and when I clucked my tongue and encouraged, "Come on, boy, let's go," he got to his feet and plodded beside me to the car. Once again he jumped into the crate when I opened it, then lay down with his head on his paws and didn't move or look up again.

I had never seen a more dispirited dog, and it just broke my heart.

Aunt Mart discouraged "shop talk" around the dinner table, but this apparently didn't apply to the pre-dinner table, because the events of yesterday were all she could talk about as we dished up peas, corn and mashed potatoes in the kitchen. "I don't think Roe slept a wink," she confided, opening the oven door a crack to check on the biscuits. "Things like this bother him more than they used to."

"Things like this would bother anyone." I opened the refrigerator and took out the covered butter dish.

"And you, honey, I don't know how you do it. Such a gruesome line of work. No, don't put the real butter on the table. Roe just slathers it all over everything. Get that stuff in the tub. High cholesterol, you know."

I traded the butter for the tub of something nondairy and nontasty. I said, "Well, I didn't know my line of work was going to be gruesome when I got into it. I thought it was going to be about fish hatcheries and preventing forest fires. And later, about teaching dogs to sit up and lie down. Dead bodies definitely did not figure into my career plan."

Aunt Mart glanced out the window to where my SUV was parked in the shade of an orange-red sweet gum tree, the back hatch open for ventilation. Hero had not made a sound, or even stirred, since lying down in the crate in the back.

"What are you going to do with the poor thing?" she worried. "I certainly hope you're not planning to keep him. You already have your hands full."

I had to agree with that. Keeping him was not even on the list of possibilities. "Hopefully, when Uncle Roe finds out who his owner was, some relative will take responsibility. Otherwise I'll try to get him into a foster home in one of the rescue groups I know."

"What this county needs is an animal shelter."

"Well, that's what we're working on." I took the bowl of three-bean salad she placed in my hands and started toward the dining room with it just as Uncle Roe appeared at the kitchen door. He was frowning a little.

"Well, so much for that," he said, inclining his head back toward the living room, where, only a moment ago, he had been talking on the phone. "That was the head of security at Letty Cranston's Hilton Head condo community, who finally got around to returning my call while we were at church. Seems she's out of the country for the winter. No itinerary, no contact info, at least not with them."

I said, "I never knew anybody that rich ever lived here."

"She moved away while you were still in high school," Aunt Mart explained. "I guess she kept the lake cabin for sentimental reasons."

I placed the salad on the table and returned for the corn. "Buck said the cabin was empty—no luggage, no purse, nothing like that. What about dog food?"

My uncle looked at me. "No," he said thoughtfully. "No people food either. No milk, no sodas, not even coffee." Then he added, "Of course, if she came up here to do herself in, she probably wouldn't have stopped for groceries on the way."

"But she should have had dog food," I argued. "When you travel with a dog, you make sure you have dog food."

Uncle Roe said, "I'll be back in a minute. I want to make some phone calls."

Aunt Mart turned from the stove in exasperation. "Roe, not on the Lord's day!"

"The Lord would approve," he assured her over his shoulder as he hurried down the hall to his den.

"We're sitting down in ten minutes with or without you!"

Ten minutes later there was enough food on the table to feed several families of three, which meant I would be dining happily on leftovers for the next few days, even after sharing with Buck. Aunt Mart was muttering to herself as she turned golden-topped biscuits into a napkin-lined basket and marched it to the table.

"Well, he can just eat his cold," she declared. "Come on in here, honey, and let's sit down. It's not like we all get to eat together every day. You think he'd show a little consideration."

I pulled out my chair just as Uncle Roe came into the room, rubbing his hands together and looking pleased with himself. He surprised me by dropping a kiss on my head before he took his own chair. "You," he said, "are a smart girl. I've got calls in to the mini-mart and the grocery store, just on the off chance somebody might remember something helpful. Then it occurred to me that maybe some city tourist with a nice purebred Lab like that wouldn't buy their dog food at a grocery store. They'd be like you, and get it at some high-priced pet store. And since the Feed and Seed is the closest thing we've got to a pet store, I just called Jeff to ask if he remembered any tourists coming in to buy dog food. Turns out somebody did come in, asking for a brand he didn't even carry. Jeff remembers because the fellow was driving a PT Cruiser, silver colored, with South Carolina plates, and they're funny-looking cars. You don't see a lot of them around here. That was on Wednesday, the day before the dog started barking enough to bother the neighbors. Fellow said he and his wife were renting a lake cabin, and they had forgotten dog food. You know Jeff, dog lover that he is. He asked what kind of dog the man had, and he said it was a yellow Lab."

I had been in the process of passing him the bread basket, but I stopped with the basket in midair. "No kidding. And you think it might be the same dog?"

Uncle Roe nodded, taking the basket from my hand. "That's exactly what I think. This woman, whoever she turns out to be, did not come up here alone. She had a husband, and we're mighty interested in finding out what became of him."

Chapter Four

When you live alone, you don't often get to sit down to a meal of roast chicken and dressing, real mashed potatoes, three kinds of vegetables and hot biscuits. Most of my meals, in fact, consist of something wrapped in a piece of bread or poured from a can, and are eaten while catching up on paperwork or returning phone calls. It takes a lot to turn my attention away from one of Aunt Mart's home-cooked meals, but this development actually caused me to abandon the spoon with which I had been about to help myself to a huge serving of crowder peas.

"Do you think maybe they had a fight and that's why she killed herself? That he left her after they got up here? How can you be sure it's the same couple?"

"'I don't know' is the answer to all of those questions," replied Uncle Roe, holding out his hand for the bowl of peas. After a moment to refocus my thoughts, I quickly took a serving for myself and passed the bowl.

"I mean, this county is crawling with tourists, and the

yellow Lab is the most popular breed in the country," I pointed out.

"Absolutely right. You going to take any of those potatoes, hon?"

I did, and he added, "I've got Buck and Wyn and half the force working on finding some answers, so don't expect him for supper tonight."

Something about the way he just assumed that Buck and I were having supper together made me a little uncomfortable, even though it was the truth. I lathered artificial butter on my biscuit. "What kind of jerk goes off and leaves his wife in a remote mountain cabin without a car *or* dog food?"

"Well, that's exactly what we need to find out, don't we?"

"I wonder if Jeff—"

My aunt set her fork down on her plate with a clink. Her plump, perfectly powdered face was stern and her eyes like flint, but nothing could have been sweeter than her voice as she remarked, "Haven't the poplars put on a show for us this season?"

Chastised, I murmured, "Sorry, Aunt Mart." And for the rest of the meal we talked about what an outstanding leaf season it had been thus far, in terms of both natural beauty and tourism, and about the trip to Myrtle Beach my aunt and uncle were planning in the spring. There were some rules for which there simply were no exceptions.

After I helped clear the table and do the dishes, I excused myself to walk the dog. He left the crate calmly when I slipped the leash around his neck, obligingly lifted his leg on a stump at the edge of the lawn when I took him there, and lapped in a desultory fashion at the water I poured into a collapsible travel bowl for him. The yard was filled with chattering squirrels, quail darting upward from the brush, chipmunks wiggling through the log pile and even a couple of insolent striped cats, but Hero wasn't interested in any of them.

He didn't look at the cats, or the birds, or the golden leaves twisting in the sun as they showered down around us. Worst of all, he didn't look at me. He just stood there at the end of the leash, his head bowed and his back to me, until I decided to try an experiment.

I said, "Hero, sit."

Without looking at me, he sat.

I was impressed. Most dogs, after even the most rudimentary lessons, are fairly reliable on the "sit" command—as long as they are standing right in front of you or beside you and are watching your body language when you say it. If you *really* want to test how well trained your dog is, give him a command while you are lying on the ground, or sitting in a chair with your back to him—or while his back is to you.

I said, "Come."

He didn't move.

A really well-trained dog will respond only to specific words, not to a beckoning tone or to generalizations such as "Come on," or "Come here." I tried again. "Here."

He got up, plodded toward me, circled behind me, and came to a stop in perfect heel position with his shoulder adjacent to my knee. I let out a breath of surprised appre-

ciation. "Good boy," I said, stroking his shoulder blades.
"Somebody's been to obedience school."

I bent down and offered my hand. "Shake," I invited.

He placed his paw in mine. "Curiouser and curiouser,"
I murmured.

I stroked under his chin, a gesture most dogs love, but
he was indifferent. I stood up. "Okay, kennel up," I said,
but made no move to lead him to the car. He turned to the
car of his own volition, leapt into the crate and lay down.

I walked thoughtfully back to the house.

"There's something strange about that dog," I said as
I came into the big, sun-filled front room. Aunt Mart was
carrying a tray filled with a coffee service and dessert
plates, and I quickly went to help her. A chocolate layer
cake was already waiting on the coffee table, displayed
beautifully on a cake plate decorated with autumn
leaves.

"He didn't try to bite you, did he?" she asked in quick
alarm, and Uncle Roe looked up from the newspaper he
was crumpling underneath the logs in the fireplace.

"No," I assured them both. "The opposite, really." I
set the tray down next to the cake, trying not to jostle the
pretty china dessert plates. "Somebody went to a lot of
trouble to train him—maybe even to competition level. I
mean, a lot of people take their dogs to obedience class,
and some people even keep up with their training so that
the dogs have good manners in public. But you just don't
see a lot of pet dogs who are so well trained that they
will obey commands even from a stranger, in an unfamil-
iar environment, under stress. It's just odd, that's all."

Uncle Roe struck a match and the newspaper caught,

sending blue and yellow flames dancing around the logs. "I don't suppose there's any way you could figure out who trained him, is there? Or where?"

I smiled regretfully. "Sorry. It's a long list."

Aunt Mart said, "I know it's early in the season to light a fire, but I just love the look of it, don't you?"

"You'll be sick and tired of it come January," said Uncle Roe, straightening up from the hearth. "And I'll be sick of chopping wood."

"I had a fire this morning," I said, remembering how nice it had been to come down and find the woodstove in the kitchen already glowing.

"Well, of course you're in the shadow of the mountain over there. It's a lot cooler."

"That cake looks wonderful, Aunt Mart." When Aunt Mart serves dessert, you don't complain about how stuffed you are from the meal, or how you're trying to lose weight, or how you really wish you'd worn a skirt with an elastic waistband. You sit down with the giant wedge she places on your plate and you count your blessings.

Uncle Roe settled down in his easy chair with his own giant wedge of cake and a cup of coffee resting on the end table at his elbow. He took a bite of the cake, complimented the baker, and then asked me, "What are you going to do with the dog?"

I gave him the same answer I had given my aunt earlier. "If the next of kin doesn't want him, or can't be found, I'll turn him over to Rescue. There are a lot of great groups out there, and as well trained as he is, he'll be a snap to place."

Uncle Roe speared another forkful of cake and nodded thoughtfully. "Meantime, I guess you'd better keep a close eye on him."

At my questioning look, he smiled. "Right now, that dog is the only one who knows what really happened up at that cabin."

I know it's silly, but I couldn't stop thinking about what Uncle Roe had said: The dog really *was* the only one who knew what had happened. He knew whether or not he had arrived in a car with a husband and a wife, and whether or not they had stopped for dog food. He knew where he came from. He knew what had happened just before the shot was fired that had taken the life of the woman in the bedroom and had begun his nightmare. It was strange, to imagine all that knowledge locked up inside the brain of a living being, but to have absolutely no way to retrieve it.

So naturally I called my friend Sonny Brightwell.

Sonny is a well-respected attorney who also happens to be an animal lover. One of the animals she loves is a sweet little border collie named Mystery, who managed to find her way to Sonny from the evil clutches of none other than Reese Pickens. That was how we had first met. But during the course of our meeting I had also discovered something else about Sonny. She claims she can communicate with animals, in particular—as far as I'm concerned—dogs.

This is what I think. Dogs are intelligent, imaginative creatures. They know how to plan, to form social relationships, to work in groups. There is even compelling scientific evidence that they dream, and they process information while dreaming in much the same way we do. And if "sentient" means self-aware, I've never known a living being more self-aware, and in fact, self-*interested*, than a dog. Do they think in the same way we do? They absolutely do not. They think *better*. They are in a dozen or more ways much more efficient, more alert, and more adapted to their environment than we are. But can they talk?

I don't think so.

That did not, however, keep Sonny from being the first person who popped into my head when I thought about Hero being the only witness to the tragedy about which there were so many questions. It wasn't that I *exactly* believed that she could talk to dogs—or rather, that they could talk to her—but if I were to be perfectly honest, I'd have to admit there had been too many coincidences concerning Sonny and the messages that she had purportedly received from animals for me to ignore. Whether it was because she was talking to them, or because of her natural empathetic personality, she did have a demonstrably calming effect on most dogs. Besides, Aunt Mart had sent home enough leftovers to feed an entire kennel club, Buck was working late and Sonny was pleasant company.

When I told her that my aunt, not I, was in charge of the kitchen, Sonny didn't hesitate to accept my invitation to supper. I'm sure the chocolate layer cake had nothing to do with it.

* * *

When introducing a new dog to the household, the best thing to do is to arrange a first meeting on neutral ground—in a park, on a street corner, or some other place where neither the resident dogs nor the new dog has a territorial stake. My version of neutral territory was the kennel play yard, which hundreds of strange dogs passed through every year, and where all of my resident dogs were accustomed to playing with visitors.

I placed Hero the Lab in the play yard and, one by one, brought out my own dogs to meet him. Part of my evaluation, before placing him with a rescue group, would be to determine how he reacted to strange dogs. His reaction was completely noncommittal. First I brought out Majesty, who is the most inoffensive dog I own, who did the whole circle-and-sniff bit while Hero just stood there stoically, ignoring her. Then I let Cisco have a turn; he was far more interested in sniffing out the aroma of chicken and dressing that clung to my hair and my clothes than he was in the stranger in the play yard. After all, he had seen them come, and he had seen them go. The Australian shepherds did their best to entice Hero to play, leaping, twirling and play-bowing, but he just gave them a long-suffering look and lay down on the ground with his head on his paws.

I had intended to keep the Lab in the boarding kennel, as was my usual custom with rescues, but something about his brokenhearted demeanor changed my mind. The other dogs obviously did not feel threatened by him, and I thought he could benefit by some hands-on inter-action inside the house. So I dragged out another big wire crate and washed and sterilized another dog bowl.

When Sonny came knocking at my door around six that evening, there were five, not four, dogs waiting to greet her. Some were better behaved than others.

The happy chaos of welcoming a visitor began with Cisco spinning and play-bowing his greeting, Majesty barking, and the Aussies bouncing from sofa to chair to floor and back while awaiting their turn to be petted; Mystery, the border collie, who accompanied Sonny everywhere she went, playfully pawed and tugged the ears of each dog who crowded around Sonny. Sonny sank quickly into a chair by the door, her long silver braid swinging over her shoulder as she bent forward with outstretched arms to give each of my pushy pets the greeting they demanded. I let this go on for about ten seconds, because Sonny would have scolded me if I had not, and then sent each of the girls to their separate crates, where they found a peanut butter–stuffed rubber toy waiting for them. Cisco, who tended to panic in small enclosed spaces like dog crates, was sent to his rug in front of the hearth, while Mystery pranced around the room picking up toys and trying to tempt him to come play. Some people might have said that was unfair to Cisco, but I thought it was good for his self-control.

Laughing, Sonny held up a bottle of wine to me. "My contribution to the meal. Maybe I should have brought dog biscuits."

In all this time, Hero, who had been lying quietly in his crate with the door open, had not moved or made a sound. As I took the wine and thanked her, Sonny noticed the newcomer. "Well," she said, rising, "who is this?"

Sonny was a tall, slim-built woman whose prematurely gray hair and porcelain skin gave her a kind of natural beauty that she never enhanced with makeup or artifice. She was probably in her fifties—only about fifteen years older than I was—but she suffered from a debilitating form of rheumatoid arthritis that sometimes was so severe it actually immobilized her. She had had a good summer and claimed a noticeable improvement in her symptoms since Mystery had come into her life. But I noticed tonight she had brought her cane and used it to balance herself as she stood. Immediately I felt a pang of chagrin for letting my dogs jump all over her.

I said, "I'm calling him Hero. We don't know his real name yet. He's just visiting."

I would tell her the full story, of course. But, I admit, I wanted to get her initial reaction to the dog before I said anything more.

She went over to the crate, and I thought she was going to bend down to pet him. It's never a good idea to invade the personal space of a strange dog, and I started to say something to that effect, but I didn't have to. She suddenly drew in her breath and straightened up, closing her eyes. I moved quickly toward her, thinking she was in pain, but she opened her eyes then and looked at me. She said, "What *happened* to this poor fellow?"

I answered cautiously, "What do you mean?"

She looked at the dog again. "Such despair," she said softly. "Oh, you poor, poor thing."

I said, hesitantly, "I don't suppose . . . I mean, you're not getting any impressions of what might have happened, are you?"

She was silent for a moment, and then I saw her repress a shudder. "Just terror, confusion and a noise like thunder. I've never known such a . . . a dark chaos. Oh, it's so sad." She looked at me gravely. "He says his life is over. Everything is all over. For heaven's sake, Raine, don't you have any idea where he came from?"

For a moment it was hard for me to speak. I had to clear my throat. "I think I'd better open the wine," I said.

As I poured the wine, I told Sonny about yesterday's gruesome find and Hero's ordeal. When I was finished, she nodded, unsurprised. "So that's the thunder I keep hearing."

It took me a moment. "Oh. The gunshot."

She sipped her wine, watching Hero from one of the two chairs I had drawn up in front of the fire. The old house was drafty, and in the winter I had all of my meals in front of a fire. "What an awful thing for him. He must have felt so helpless, being locked outside the door."

"I don't even like to think about the kind of person who could do something like that."

"We can never know another person's heart, Raine. She must have been very deeply disturbed."

I suppose she was right, but I couldn't seem to find much sympathy for the deceased under the circumstances. I was spared from answering by the distant sound of the oven timer. I took a quick sip of my wine and set the glass on the occasional table. "Be right back."

"Do you need any help?"

"No, just relax." I grinned. "Even I can manage paper plates and leftovers."

A beseeching look from the hearth rug was Cisco's

way of reminding me what a very good dog he had
been—particularly considering the fact that Mystery had
settled down not three feet away from him with one of
his favorite toys—so I said, in passing, "Okay, boy, release."

And then the oddest thing happened. Predictably,
Cisco bounded to his feet and went straight for the toy
with which Mystery was teasing him. But at the same
time, Hero emerged from his crate just as though he too
were responding to the word "release." He stood there
for a moment, looking confused. Sonny extended her
hand to him and called his name softly, but he didn't
even glance at her. He turned around and went back into
his crate.

I shook my head helplessly and continued to the
kitchen.

"I've been kind of working with him," I explained to
Sonny as we settled with our plates of warmed-over
chicken and dressing at the little table I'd drawn up before the fire. "Just trying to see how responsive he is, you
know. The thing is, I think someone really put some time
into training this dog. For one thing, look."

I gestured toward the canine population that surrounded us. Cisco, the dog in whom I had invested
countless hours of training, lay obediently at my feet, his
eyes fixed upon my fork, long strings of drool hanging
from his jowls. Begging at the table is, by any other
name, still begging. Mystery was a bit more subtle about
it. She sat prettily a few feet away, but the way she
watched every bite Sonny took indicated that she was by
no means a stranger to the good things that come from

human plates. Even my three crated dogs were sitting at attention, rubber bones forgotten, hoping for a morsel to be tossed their way. But Hero lay quietly in his crate with the door open, indifferent to tantalizing aromas and the other dogs' interest, while we enjoyed our meal. That was the way a dog with perfect manners was supposed to behave.

Sonny pointed out, "He's probably too depressed to be interested in food."

"Well, there's that," I agreed. "But watch this."

Without getting up from the table, I said, "Hero, here."

Hero slowly got out of his crate and came over to me. Ignoring both Mystery and Cisco, who were actually distracted enough from their fixation upon the plates of food to turn and sniff him as he passed, Hero sat beside my chair.

I said, "Down."

He shifted his weight to one hip and lay down.

"Roll over," I said.

The dog obligingly showed his belly.

"Impressive," agreed Sonny, raising an eyebrow. "And if he does all this for a stranger, imagine how well he'd perform for the person who actually trained him."

"Exactly," I said. I knew she would understand. "It's not every day you meet a dog like this."

To Hero I said, "Release," and he got to his feet.

He started to go back to his crate, but Sonny stretched out her hand. "Come here, sweet boy."

"Don't feed him from the table," I warned, unnecessarily.

Hero turned his head toward Sonny's outstretched hand and sniffed it disinterestedly. She ran her hand over his big, blocky head, tugging at his ear. He tolerated her petting, but did not respond to it. Mystery, however, was starting to look annoyed, so I said, "It's probably better not to give him too much attention while we're eating. We don't want to start a dogfight."

"That's the last thing this poor guy needs," agreed Sonny, and then she hesitated. "Wait a minute. What's this?"

Her gentle stroking had pushed one of his floppy ears backward, and even from my seat across from her I could see a darkish smudge against the pale pink under-skin of his ear. I left my chair and sank down to my knees to examine it.

"It's a tattoo," I said, looking up at her.

She looked as surprised as I felt. "A tattoo? Who tattoos their dog's ear?"

"Actually," I said slowly, "it used to be a fairly common practice before microchipping. People with field champions, expensive breed stock, any kind of valuable dog, wanted to be able to identify it if the dog was stolen."

"Good heavens. Is that what he is, then, do you think? A field champion?"

I shook my head. "I don't think so. Hardly anybody tattoos anymore." I didn't think it was necessary to add that the reason the practice had been mostly abandoned was because thieves had discovered that the simplest way to eliminate a tattooed dog's identification was to cut off its ear.

"Well, obviously somebody does."

My heart was beginning to pound with excitement. "Some laboratories," I admitted, "who do research on domestic animals. A few police departments, but none around here. And"—I slid my arm around Hero's neck as I looked up at Sonny, suddenly filled with certainty— "service dog organizations."

Chapter Five

There are dozens upon dozens of agencies in the United States that supply service dogs to people who are blind or otherwise disabled, and all of them do remarkable work. Most of them actually retain legal ownership of the dogs they train even after they are placed with a person with a disability, and perform regular follow-up visits to make sure the match is still going well. All of them keep excellent records.

I started calling as soon as anyone could reasonably be expected to be in the office Monday morning, and I was a bit disappointed when the two biggest agencies, Leader Dogs for the Blind and Canine Companions for Independence, both reported that the tattoo number I read off was not one of theirs. After that, I decided to concentrate on agencies in the Southeast. On the fifth try—Coastal Assistance Dogs, in Mount Pleasant, South Carolina—I hit pay dirt.

The man who came to the phone after I had been put on hold sounded friendly but concerned. "Miss Stockton," he said, "my name is Wes Richards. I understand you've found one of our dogs?" That last part seemed to hold a note of skepticism, as though he didn't want to accuse me of misrepresenting myself, but could hardly believe one of *his* dogs was actually lost.

I sat up from the slumped position I had taken in my chair at the kennel office, instantly alert and revitalized. "Your dogs?" I repeated. "Then he is one of yours? That's your tattoo number?"

"His name is Nero," replied Wes, "a four-year-old yellow Lab, neutered, approximately sixty-five pounds, tattoo number 6520034. Is that correct?"

"That's him," I said, and released a huge sigh of relief. "Thank goodness." *Nero.* That explained why he had appeared to respond to his name when I called him Hero. Although dogs can eventually learn to recognize hundreds of very specific words and associate their meanings, names for them are just sounds. Nero and Hero, to a dog, sound almost exactly the same.

"But I'm afraid I don't understand. You said you found him? Ms. White has been an excellent partner for Nero and I can't imagine him leaving her under any circumstances. I just checked our overnight messages and there was nothing about Nero being missing. Could you tell me where he was found?"

I set down the coffee cup from which I had been about to take a self-congratulatory sip, wincing at the unpleasant duty I now had to perform. I said, "He didn't leave her, Mr. Richards. At least not on purpose."

As briefly as I could, I described how the yellow Lab

had ended up with me. There was a shocked silence when I finished.

Finally he murmured, "How . . . dreadful. I don't think anyone here would have guessed that she was unstable. . . . I mean, of course no one did, or we never would have placed the dog. We have very high standards. I just . . . don't know what to say."

"The police will be calling you for information on the owner. Up until now, we haven't had any way of identifying her."

"Oh," he said distractedly. "Yes, of course, whatever you need. Her name was Michelle White. Everyone called her Mickey. We're a small agency, Miss Stockton, and we keep very close track of our placements. We require them to come in once a year for evaluation and what we like to call fine-tuning of the training." Now that he was talking about dogs, not death, his voice began to take on more confidence. I understood this completely.

"You know, as a team works together they discover certain quirks or peculiarities, and sometimes the handler will develop special needs that we try to address by refining a behavior or even teaching a whole new set of behaviors. The relationship between a person with disabilities and his dog is an ever-changing, ever-evolving one, and at Coastal Assistance Dogs we provide ongoing support." He seemed to stop himself. "I'm sorry, I'm afraid I'm rambling. You're not interested in all that. It's all just—such a shock."

"I'm very interested," I told him. "I'm a dog trainer myself. Mostly search and rescue, and some local therapy dog work. I've never tried anything as complicated as training a service dog, though."

"Our dogs are in training for two years before we place them," he explained, seeming to relax again now that he knew he was talking to a "dog" person. "Then we work with the handler and the dog one-on-one for up to six weeks before we send them home, depending on the needs of the person with whom we're placing the dog. For the first year, we do home visits every three months, and after that we ask the team to return to the training center for evaluation once a year."

"When was Mickey White last in?"

I could hear the tapping of a keyboard. "August," he said after a moment. "And there's absolutely no notation here that either the trainer or the social worker noticed anything out of the ordinary. She was very happy with Nero, and Nero was working out even better than we had hoped. Of course, she understood that as her condition continued to deteriorate, she would depend on her dog more and more, and it was very important that we continue to refine his training."

"She had a deteriorating condition?" I said, wondering whether the deterioration had been progressing faster than she had expected, and whether that had led to the despair that caused her to pull the trigger. "Can you tell me what it was?"

He hesitated. "Technically, our records are private."

I said, "I understand. I was just wondering about the kinds of things the dog learned to do for her. Was she completely dependent on her chair?"

He answered, "She used a chair most of the time, but

so far the paralysis had affected only one side. As a trained service dog, though, Nero was able to perform just about any task she might need—from helping to take off her shoes to turning on light switches, picking up dropped items, carrying purchases, even bringing medicine bottles and bottled water. He was thoroughly reliable."

"Wow," I said. "That explains a lot." Then, "What is your policy about the dogs? I mean, what will happen to him now? Does he go to the next of kin, or what?"

"He will return to us," Wes assured me, "as per our contract with Ms. White. He'll be retrained, and hopefully placed with someone else. Where did you say you were?"

I told him.

"I can probably have a volunteer drive out to pick him up this coming weekend," Wes said. "If it's a problem for you to keep him until then—"

"No, it's not a problem. What's one more?"

"Generally we'd ask you to just put him on a plane but—"

"No planes fly between here and there," I assured him. "Really, it's okay."

"I'll call you back with the details as soon as I have them. Meanwhile, if you'll give me your fax number, I can send you some information about him—his diet, his command words, that sort of thing."

"That would be great." I read off the number.

"I really appreciate your help with this, Miss Stockton, not only for taking care of Nero but for going to all the trouble of tracking us down. He's a very special dog, and we'd hate to lose him."

I said, "It was my pleasure. I've been calling him Hero." I added, "I thought it was odd that he seemed to respond. I guess that's because it sounds like his real name."

"I doubt he can distinguish such a subtle difference."

"Just as long as I don't do any permanent damage by calling him by the wrong name."

"I think the fact that he responds at all is a testament to his excellent training."

"I agree."

I was about to bring the conversation to an end when something occurred to me. "Mr Richards, you said Mickey White was paralyzed on one side. Do you happen to know which side it was?"

He answered, "Yes, I do, actually. It was her right side."

I hung up the phone slowly, unable to rid my mind of the picture of those swollen fingers and the gun lying on the floor just beneath them. If Mickey White was paralyzed on her right side, how had she shot herself with her right hand?

I picked up the phone again and dialed the sheriff's office.

Maude came in just as I hung up the phone. Cisco, who had been entertaining himself in the front kennel run, came bouncing in with her and launched his paws onto the front of the desk in search of treats. I said, "You won't believe this. He's a service dog!"

Maude glanced at Cisco as she removed her plaid barn coat and hung it on a hook. "That one? Not bloody likely."

I gave Cisco a stern look and he dropped all four paws to the floor, grinning.

"No, Hero. The Lab. I found a tattoo in his ear last night. I finally linked him up with Coastal Assistance Dogs just a few minutes ago."

"Good work," said Maude, impressed. "And of course they were able to identify his owner."

I nodded. "Her name was Mickey White. The police will have to go through the identification procedures, but it's starting to look like this might not have been a suicide."

Cisco went over to the toy basket, grabbed a stuffed elephant and brought it to me, tail swishing. Maude raised an eyebrow. "Really?"

"She was in a wheelchair," I explained, "and paralyzed on one side. Anyway, the state medical examiner has the body, and Uncle Roe says they should know something by the afternoon."

I took the toy elephant from Cisco's mouth and placed it on the desk. He returned to the basket.

Maude said, "It looks as though someone would have mentioned finding a wheelchair in the cabin. And where was the dog's harness?"

"Not to mention her car," I added. "Uncle Roe thinks she may have come up here with her husband." Briefly, while extracting yet another toy from Cisco's mouth, I explained the conversation with Jeff at the Feed and Seed.

"I can well imagine that this husband, if that's who he turns out to be, is a person of great interest to the police at this moment."

I nodded. "But what doesn't make sense to me—"

My words were cut off by a concussion of gunfire— *Pow! Pow!*—that was loud enough to cause Cisco to drop his latest treasure and almost made me tip over backward in my chair.

"I swear to—"

Again, gunshots cut off my words. Cisco ran to the window and jumped up with his paws on the sill, barking frantically. From behind the concrete walls that separated the office from the kennel area, more than a dozen canine voices joined in.

Maude said matter-of-factly, "I meant to tell you, I think I spotted the culprits as I came in. Their vehicle is parked at the bottom of the old logging trail across the road. I suspect they've got a deer stand in Granny's Meadow somewhere."

Granny's Meadow was a creek-side glade about five hundred feet up the mountain—and less than a rifle shot away from my back door. I said, "Cisco, quiet!"

When he didn't even glance over his shoulder at me, I got to my feet and marched over to him, taking him firmly by the collar. I gasped when I saw what he was barking at. "Oh, my God!"

It was Hero. Somehow he had escaped the house and was making a mad dash around the yard. How had he gotten out? What had happened?

I flew out the door and into the yard, slipping on the colorful carpet of dried leaves as I raced across the ex-

panse of ground between the kennel and the house. The
yellow Lab was lunging in a frenetic zigzag pattern between the front porch of the house and the chain-link
fences that enclosed both the backyard and the side kennel area. His tongue was lolling, his eyes were wild and
his muzzle was flecked with foam. There were dark
streaks on both his forelegs and he was clearly in the grip
of a panic attack. Right now he was running because he
was trapped and running was all he knew how to do, but
it was only a matter of time before he discovered, by accident or intent, that the fences did not meet. All he had
to do was turn the other way, and he would be racing toward the highway.

A golden blur of barking frenzy sailed past me, heading toward the terrified Lab. All I needed was a dogfight—or, worse, for the two of them to take off together
to parts unknown. I skidded on a pile of leaves as I
grabbed for Cisco's collar and ended up on my hands
and knees. But before I hit the ground, years of dog
training instinct took over and I bellowed, *"Down!"*

"Come" is a good command to know in an emergency, as long as it is absolutely, one hundred percent
reliable. "Down" is a better one. A dog who is moving—
even if he's moving toward you—can still get hit by a
car, bitten by a snake, or attacked by another dog. A dog
who responds to the command "down" well enough to
drop to the ground in midstride and remain motionless
until told otherwise will very likely one day save his own
life.

Fortunately, Cisco was as well trained as I was. We
had practiced this a hundred thousand times for fun and

food, and as far as he was concerned, this was just another game. He dropped to the ground a few yards ahead of me, grinning delightedly and panting with exertion and excitement.

And so, to my amazement, did the Labrador retriever.

Maude was beside me before I could even release a breath of relief. A quick glance told her I was okay, so she barely broke stride as she continued toward the Lab. I was half a step behind her.

"Good, Cisco, good. Down," I said breathlessly, and I flicked him a treat from my pocket as I bent to ruffle his ears. "Great dog! Good job! Now, stay."

He looked disappointed but brightened when I tossed him another treat as I hurried off.

Maude was kneeling beside the yellow Lab, gently examining his forelimbs as she murmured reassuring words. I could see his convulsive shivers as I approached, and when I dropped down on the other side of him, I realized that the dark streaks on his legs were blood.

"Oh, Hero, I'm so sorry, boy. What happened? Are you okay?" I looked at Maude in anguish. "I should have brought him to the kennel with me, but he seemed fine with the other dogs, and I wasn't going to be gone long. Do you think it was a fight? Is he okay? How did he get out of the house?"

"Just a scratch," Maude said briskly. "A little peroxide will do the trick just fine. Don't baby him, Raine, you're only reinforcing his fear."

I knew that, but it's hard *not* to pet and comfort a dog who is lying prostrate on the ground, sides heaving, wracked with shivers. Besides, wasn't it she who had been murmuring good-dog talk to him when I first came up?

I repeated, "What happened?" I wasn't sure whether I addressed the question to her or to Hero, but when I followed the direction of Maude's pointed gaze, I knew the answer.

Glass glittered on the front porch beneath one of the windows, and a breeze sucked the edge of one of my mother's lace curtains through the newly formed opening. "Oh, my God," I said softly, "He jumped through the window."

Maude gently slipped a loop leash over the dog's head. "Poor thing. He must be gun-shy."

I looked at her grimly. "Wouldn't you be?"

I got to my feet. "Can you take care of him?"

"Of course. But—"

"I'll be right back."

I called, "Cisco, load up," as I strode to my car, and less than thirty seconds later Cisco and I were barreling down the dirt drive at a speed that left plumes of dust in our wake.

A sleek black Range Rover was parked just off the highway on the old logging road, just as Maude had described it. I pulled up beside it and got out of my car, slamming the door. I marched over to the Range Rover and grabbed the door handle, hoping to set off the security alarm. But the fool who owned it hadn't even locked it, and the door swung open at my tug. In retrospect, I think this was probably a good thing, because my next move was going to be to smash out the window with a rock. Sometimes I have a temper.

I reached inside and leaned on the horn with all my weight. I kept up the loud, steady, wailing pressure while Cisco scrambled to the front seat of my car and, propping his front paws on the dashboard, joined in the cacophony with a chorus of alert, excited barking. I kept up the pressure until my arm began to ache and I had to shift my weight to maintain my balance on the rocky ground. I would happily have kept it up until I ran the car battery down, but after what was probably no more than four minutes there was a crashing in the undergrowth where the logging road disappeared into the woods, and two men came rushing and stumbling out of the shadows.

They were dressed like models in an L.L.Bean catalog, in tan corduroy hunting jackets with leather-trimmed pockets and flannel-lined caps with the earflaps turned up. They carried their rifles aloft like spears, waving them madly to keep their balance when they skidded on dead leaves or tripped over vines. I abruptly released the pressure on the horn, my jaw dropping in astonishment. Any ten-year-old around here knows you never carry a rifle in anything other than breach position—broken over your arm—and you most certainly never, ever run through the woods with a loaded gun. I felt as though I ought to duck.

One of them, an overweight, red-faced man, came huffing and puffing across the lane toward me, shouting, "What the hell is going on here? Get away from that car!" The other, leaner and bespectacled but obviously in no better shape, struggled to keep up.

Cisco barked sharply and excitedly through the partially lowered window of my vehicle. There was nothing he loved better than an adrenaline rush first thing in the morning. The two men, noticing him, and taking stock of me as I stepped back from behind the open door of the Range Rover, slowed their frantic pace a little. But the red-faced one did not look any less annoyed just because he had discovered the vandal to be a woman with a dog.

"What is the meaning of this?" he demanded.

I said the first thing that came to my mind. "Do you have a current hunting license?"

He looked taken aback, and his companion, just then coming abreast of him, gasped, "Is there—a problem here?"

The slight wheeze to his breathing suggested an asthmatic who had no business being out here amidst all this leaf mold, much less traversing rugged countryside with a gun. My contempt became mitigated by pity, but not enough to overcome my anger. Before I could snap back a reply, another man emerged from the woods. He wore his jacket open and his gun slung over his shoulder on a strap, which demonstrated that he might possess a modicum more intelligence than his companions, and he strode rather than ran. But he was every bit as city smooth and woods stupid as his two cohorts.

He was scowling as he came toward us. "What's going on here, Jack?"

Cisco barked a greeting to the newcomer and the scowl cleared as he looked from the big, bouncing golden retriever inside the SUV to me. He said, "Is something wrong?"

The heavy one said, "She wants to see our hunting license!"

The newcomer raised an eyebrow. Even without seeing the smooth Caribbean tan and the two-hundred-dollar haircut, I would have recognized the authority of a man who was accustomed to being in charge—and to having things his way, when he wanted them, and without asking twice.

He fixed me with a cool gray gaze and inquired politely, "And who might you be?"

Of course by then I realized I was in over my head, but I never have known when to give up and start swimming for shore. So I squared my shoulders, met his eyes and replied, "I'm Raine Stockton, from the Hanson Point Ranger Station."

His expression relaxed as he looked me up and down, obviously making note of my tattered barn jacket and dusty jeans, not a badge or a uniform in sight. He said, "That's the forest service, isn't it?"

I felt my cheeks color. I hated that. "That's right."

"Aren't hunting licenses issued by the fish and game commission?"

I glared at him. "That doesn't mean you don't have to have one."

"True enough. But it does make me wonder what interest you would have in seeing it."

"I didn't ask to see it," I snapped back at him. "I just asked if you had one."

At that point the bespectacled man stepped forward, still wheezing, and held out three pieces of creased paper. I recognized the seal of the fish and game commission and brushed the papers away. "Because if you *did* have licenses," I went on hotly, "any of you, I was going to petition my state representative for a change in the law—one that does not allow for the issuing of hunting licenses to complete idiots!"

Cisco, always eager to cheer me on, punctuated my sentiment with a bark from the window. The stranger glanced at him and smiled, and then surprised me by extending his hand to me. I recognized, from my last trip to the Asheville Mall, the scent of Ralph Lauren's Polo for Men. "Miles Young, Miss Stockton. This is Jack Crane, my architect, and George Williams, my attorney. Reese Pickens told me you were a pistol. Good to see the old coot didn't lie about one thing."

It took me far too long to put all of this together. I just stood there, glaring at him, ignoring his hand until he shrugged and dropped it.

"I own this mountain," he explained. "I'm your new neighbor."

I felt a chill go through me, synchronized with a sinking sensation in the pit of my stomach, as all the signs I should have previously read came together into one incontrovertible conclusion. The powerful-looking, overdressed, mildly handsome—in a sleazy kind of way—completely inept woodsman with spiky hair and buffed nails was the man who was single-handedly responsible for desecrating a mountain landscape that had remained unchanged for thousands of years; for destroying the habitats of uncounted wildlife; for threatening the watershed; for bringing petrochemicals and smog and, worse yet, the idle rich into our pristine little corner of wilderness, leaving it desolate and forever altered.

The thing is, until I actually stood there staring at him—whitened teeth, flawless pores and all—I don't think I entirely believed any of it was real. He gave it a name, a face, a presence. Until now the future had seemed to be a mere threat. Suddenly it was an inevitability.

I said, unaccountably and with all the contempt I could muster, "No real hunter would wear cologne. You smell like a department store."

He grinned. "Thank you. And as you might have guessed, this isn't a real hunting trip. We're more or less just getting the lay of the land. And of course"—the tip of his head, the deepening of his smile, seemed more of an insult than a courtesy—"meeting the neighbors."

I looked at him for another moment, and as I stood there even the bright autumn sunlight seemed to grow cold and brittle. Then I said simply, "No, Mr. Young. You're not my neighbor. Neighbors bring you soup when you're sick and call when you've got troubles and fix your fence posts without being asked. You're just a greedy stranger trying to make money off of something you don't understand and can never be a part of."

I walked around my car and opened the driver's door. "You're shooting too close to my house," I told him flatly. "You do it again and I'll have the sheriff out here, I don't care how many lawyers you've got sweeping up after you."

There was an odd look in his eye as he watched me get behind the wheel, as though he were not so much angry as intrigued. He said, "Oh, don't worry, Miss Stockton. The hunting party is over. Tomorrow we bring in the bulldozers."

I slammed the door, started the engine and threw it into reverse. They had to scramble to get out of the way, and I came close enough to clipping the side of the Range Rover that the architect actually swore at me. Cisco barked at him indignantly, and that arrogant SOB Young actually grinned and raised his hand in a wave. I left him in a cloud of dust and didn't look back.

Chapter Six

"Well, damn, sweetie," Buck said, tapping a nail into the piece of plywood that covered the hole in my window, "I hope I'm not going to have to go beat this guy up. This is a clean shirt."

Buck is one of the mildest men I know. He's a lot like my uncle in that way, and I'm not saying that mildness is not an excellent characteristic in a law officer. But sometimes it's so annoying I just want to pinch him.

"He grinned at Cisco," I muttered, scowling.

"Well, now, that's grounds for hanging in my book." Buck reached down and scratched my golden retriever's ears, and Cisco grinned back up at him.

I sat cross-legged on the floor beside Hero's crate, lightly stroking the Lab's blocky head while he dozed. His wounds had been cleaned and, as Maude had predicted, were barely more than scratches. She had immediately given him a dose of Rescue Remedy—a holistic blend of flower essences in a strong alcohol base that almost every dog trainer has used at one time or another to soothe a stressed dog (although I personally think its effects may have more to do with the alcohol than the flowers)—and now that the gunfire had stopped, he was resting comfortably.

"Poor old fellow," Buck observed, positioning another nail. "It's a wonder he didn't slice open an artery."

"I'll keep him locked in his crate from now on when I'm not with him," I said. "I've got a call in to that guy at Coastal Assistance Dogs, but looks like he would have told me if the dog was noise sensitive. I mean that's always the first thing I mention to people when I'm placing a rescue dog in a new home, if they have a problem like that."

"I can't imagine that any reputable agency would pair a woman in a wheelchair with a service dog who jumps through windows when he hears a loud noise."

"Me either." I sighed, untangling a tiny knot from the fine fur behind Hero's ear. "I suspect this is a recent development." I looked up at him. "So do you know anything more about what she was doing here or"—a slight, respectful hesitation—"how she died?"

He drove the nail home with two hammer blows. "The body has been turned over to the state medical examiner. We expect him to confirm what you—or rather, what the service dog people—told us. And if Mickey White was paralyzed on her right side, the cause of death was obviously not suicide."

"And the husband . . ."

"Leo White," Buck confirmed. "Definitely a person of interest. She was also survived by a father in Chattanooga. The Mount Pleasant police are working with us, trying to get some information on what might have be-come of the husband. They confirm, by the way, that she owned a silver PT Cruiser."

"So it *was* them who stopped at the Feed and Seed for dog food."

"Jeff can't confirm the wife was in the car," Buck pointed out. "He only talked to the husband."

I stroked the velvety line along the Labrador's nose. "It just seems so strange to me. A service dog's job is to be at his handler's side twenty-four, seven. How did Hero get locked outside the bedroom while the killer— well, did what he did?"

"Another thing that points to the husband. Seems to me that if you lived with a dog like that, and you knew that his job was to serve and, well, protect, your victim, the first thing you would do is make sure he couldn't do his job."

"I suppose."

Cisco came over to me and nudged his head under my arm, a rather blatant attempt to divert my attention away from the Lab and onto a more deserving dog—such as himself. I patted his head absently with my free hand.

Buck drove home the final nail and stepped back from the project. "That ought to keep the wind out till T.J. gets over here this afternoon with a new windowpane. Tell him to caulk and paint those nail holes too, will you? I used finishing nails so they wouldn't scar the wood."

"I'll tell you something else that bothers me," I said. I elbowed Cisco away as he started to become a pest. "No wheelchair, no harness for the service dog, not even a water bowl. I mean, what did he do, carry her inside, lock the dog out of the bedroom, shoot her and drive away? And if that was his plan, why did he let the dog in the house in the first place? Why not just dump the service dog on the side of the road as he was making his getaway? And why stop for dog food?"

Buck said, "Murder is a crime of passion, sweetheart. And crimes of passion don't always have to make sense."

"Then why did he just happen to bring a handgun on vacation with him?"

"Nobody 'just happens' to bring a handgun anywhere."

"Exactly."

"But last I checked, we didn't have any information on the gun, it being the weekend and all. And of course we didn't know we were looking at a murder until a couple of hours ago."

Cisco trotted across the room, dug a tennis ball out from under an easy chair and returned to me with it, tail wagging madly.

I said, "No luck locating the car, I guess."

"Five hundred miles of road in this county alone," Buck pointed out, "not to mention trails, paths and driveways that lead nowhere. It might take a while."

Cisco dropped the ball at my feet and, when I ignored him, he nudged my arm insistently with his nose. I ignored that too. You never want to get into the habit of letting your dog tell you what to do, even if all he wants you to do is play ball.

"He probably left the car in a parking lot somewhere across the state line and stole another one," I observed.

"You should have been a cop." Buck scooped up the ball and bounced it across the room for Cisco to chase.

I grimaced at him. "If I were a cop, I certainly would have given Mr. Miles Young more than a piece of my mind this morning."

Cisco skidded to a stop at Buck's feet with the tennis ball in his mouth. Buck pried the ball from his teeth and tossed it again. "I'll talk to him if you want me to, but you know as well as I do that there's no law against a man hunting on his own land during hunting season."

"I just feel sorry for this guy," I said, rubbing Hero's ears. "I'm not even going to be able to keep him until the end of the week if this keeps up—not to mention what it's doing to the kennel dogs. Of course, Young did say his hunting party was over. Said he was bringing in bulldozers, like that was going to scare me."

Buck frowned, the soggy tennis ball poised for another toss. "What did Sonny say?"

The big Lab stretched out his forelegs and sighed in his sleep, and I rested a hand on his head. "She said the poor thing was too traumatized to remember anything. Not surprising, since he's practically too traumatized to eat."

Buck gave me a puzzled look. Cisco sat expectantly in front of him, eyes fixed upon the tennis ball, tail swishing along the floor. He said, "I meant about the bulldozers."

"Oh." I should mention that Sonny, in addition to being a dog lover and possible pet psychic, is a world-class environmental attorney who was spearheading the efforts of the Save the Mountains group to stop the development of Hawk Mountain. Or at least that was the goal. As Sonny had recently explained to me, these things are rarely ever *stopped*. The most one can hope for is that they can be managed.

"She said they've come to a maximum-density agreement, whatever that means, and a promise for an eco-friendly golf course," I replied glumly. "Whoopee."

"Well, that's something. At least they're willing to talk." He tossed the ball again and Cisco scrambled.

"What kind of man wears Polo to go deer hunting anyway?"

Buck looked confused. "Polo? You mean the shirt?"

"No, the cologne. He probably scared away every deer in the county smelling like that."

An odd look. "You noticed how he smelled?"

"Couldn't help it. Don't throw the ball in the house, Buck. You're going to break a lamp."

"I think I'd better go to work."

"Yeah, me too." I got to my feet. "Maude had to run into town for kennel cleaner and nobody's minding the phone in the office. Thanks for fixing the window."

He brushed my hair with a kiss. "See you for dinner?"

"Are you cooking?"

"What happened to my leftovers?"

I shrugged defensively. "You snooze, you lose around here. Besides, nothing is good the second day."

"Thanks a lot."

"There might be some cake left," I suggested as he headed for the door.

"Something tells me I'd better pick it up on the way out if I want any."

"Good plan," I agreed. "Call me about dinner."

I gently closed and latched the gate on Hero's kennel and slapped my thigh for Cisco, who was gazing rather disconsolately toward the door by which Buck had just left. "Come on, boy," I said. "Let's go to work."

According to the machine's blinking LED reader, there were three messages waiting for me when I reached the kennel office. The first one was nothing but static. The second one was a hang up. The third one began, "Maudie, *darling*, thank heavens, these phones are just the *worst*! Got your message, love, dying to talk. The number here is—"

And a dial tone.

I punched replay, and at that moment the phone rang. "Dog Daze," I answered.

The voice, and the words, were such an exact match for the ones I had heard on the answering machine that I blinked in confusion, looking from the answering machine to the telephone, before I could focus on the fact that it was a live person who was speaking.

"Maudie, darling, thank goodness! These phones are just the pits! It's Letty, darling, calling all the way from Crete, can you believe it? What in the world is going on back there? First I get all these messages from the Hanover County Sheriff's Department, and then you call, and—oh, my dear, are you all right? Talk to me!"

Letty. Crete. I made the connection this time a lot more quickly than I had done with Miles Young and the hunting party on the mountain. "Mrs. Cranston, this is Raine Stockton."

"Oh, no! Do I have the wrong number?"

"No," I assured her quickly, "I'm Maude's business partner. She's not here right now, but I know what she was calling you about—"

"Do I know you, dear? Are you related to that Judge Stockton from up around there?"

"He's my father," I said, wondering how much it cost per minute to call Hanover County from Crete.

"Is that a fact? How is the old scoundrel, anyway?"

"Well," I said, hesitating, "actually he passed away some years back."

"Oh, my. Did I know that? Seems I should have known that. But it's been so long since I was back that way. I keep meaning to come up there and spend a few weeks at the lake every summer, but there are so *many* places in this world to go, don't you know, it's hard to get to them all. I still have that cute little cabin up there that William built for me—oh, it must have been thirty-five years ago now. I'll bet a lot has changed since then, though, hasn't it? We were practically in the wilderness back in those days! But I keep getting a bill from the management company every year for maintenance, so I guess the place is still standing. I rent it out sometimes, just so that I can have someone in there. I think houses need to be lived in, don't you? I have a lovely couple who house-sits for me in Montana when I'm not out there and it makes all the difference in the world. I wish I could find someone to stay at the house in Florida, but it's so hard to find anyone reliable. I declare, I don't suppose you would know anyone who might be interested, would you?"

Finally, she paused for breath and I was able to inter-ject a word. "Mrs Cranston, about your cabin—"

"Oh, dear, if you were calling about renting it, I'm afraid it's taken for the season. A nice young couple from South Carolina. She's in a wheelchair, don't you know—"

By now I had figured that the only way to talk to her was to interrupt, so I said, "For the season? Do you mean until the end of the year?"

The silence on the other end seemed a little offended, and I wondered whether interrupting her might not have been a good idea after all. "My dear, of course not. I mean until the end of *leaf* season. Why on earth would anyone want to be up there after November?"

"Did the Whites rent the cabin for the whole month, then?" And how could you go away for a whole month without remembering the dog food?

"Oh, do you know Mickey and Leo, then?"

"Not really, but—"

"What business did you say you were in, dear? Real estate?"

"No, dogs."

"I'm sorry? This connection is breaking down."

"I said I'm a dog trainer," I repeated, more loudly. "Boarding too. But this really isn't about—"

"Did you say dogs? You couldn't have said dogs. Why in the world are you calling me about dogs?"

"Maude was calling you," I reminded her, "and what she wanted was—"

"Because I've only owned one dog in my life, and it's been dead for years. Bichon frise. Can't say I was sorry to see him go. Wouldn't eat anything but tuna. Hated the cat. Disgraced himself on my Manolo Blahniks. Horrid creature. What did you—"

A burst of static.

I said quickly, "Is there a number where Maude can—"

"Tell her I enjoyed our chat—" Static. "Call when I—" Static, static, and nothing.

I shouted, "Hello? Hello?" a few times, to no avail. I stared at the dead receiver in frustration, and then returned it to its stand. It rang again almost immediately. I snatched it up.

"Hello, Mrs. Cranston?"

A hesitation. "Raine, is that you? This is Dolly Amstead."

I grimaced. "Hi, Dolly. Sorry, I was expecting someone else."

"Well, I won't keep you." Her voice was crisp and efficient. "I just wanted to go over this list with you to make sure everything is all set for this weekend."

This weekend. My grimace deepened. The volunteer from Coastal Assistance Dogs was supposed to pick up Hero this weekend. There was certainly no way I was going to be able to get out of my obligation at the Pet Fair—nor would I dare try—so I would just have to ask whoever was coming for the dog to meet me there.

I said, "Everything's all set, really. You don't have to worry about a thing."

"Nonetheless, let's just go over it again, shall we? Now, do you have someone to transport the equipment you need?"

I sighed, resigned to another endless half hour of Dolly's lists. "I do. We'll be there by seven to set up."

"Very good. I have you scheduled for an agility demonstration at nine thirty, and then we'll start selling tickets to let people try it with their own dogs. Two dollars each, right? And who do you have to take the money?"

In the dictionary beside the word "micromanager" there is a picture of Dolly Amstead. I suppressed a sigh. "Maude is going to help man the booth."

"Oh, dear." She sounded concerned. "I have her down to do an obedience demo at ten thirty. I just don't see how she can help with your booth and be ready for the demo by then. There's bound to be some overlap. And I can't move the obedience demo, because I have the dancing dog at eleven."

"The dancing *what*?"

"Oh, Raine, I told you about that! That girl from Charleston—what's her name?—wait, I have it here. . . ." Keyboard tapping. "Lanier. Sandra Lanier. She does this all over the Carolinas to raise money for humane shelters and whatnot. She sent me a tape, and it's the cutest thing you've ever seen. The dog jumps through her arms and over her legs and does a little cha-cha and actually looks like he's dancing. She called it canine musical something."

"Freestyle," I supplied, understanding. I had read about it and noticed it on the Internet, but had never actually seen it in person. "I didn't know there was anyone around here doing that."

"Well, she's not from around here, exactly, is she? And we were lucky to get her. It just so happened that she was planning a hiking trip here next week anyway."

This time of year there were more cars with South

Carolina license plates cruising our roads than there were with North Carolina ones, and most of them were from the coast. Dolly wasn't really as lucky as she thought; with all the tourists flooding our mountains, who knew what kind of talent we might find if we just put out the call?

"At any rate," Dolly went on, "I'm going to have to try to find you another volunteer, because there simply is no way I can change the schedule now. Now, let's go over the lineup for—"

At that moment, blessedly, my pager began to beep. As a member of Mountain Search and Rescue, I am supposed to wear the pager at all times, but the truth is, I only think about it right after a drill or during peak tourist season. Today, I hadn't actually even put the thing on; I had just tossed it into the in-basket on my desk, where it was now squeaking irritably.

I said, quickly, "Sorry, Dolly, that's an emergency page. Gotta go."

I hung up as she was still sputtering and glanced at the number on the digital screen, even though I already knew what it would be. I dialed the ranger station from memory.

"What's up?" I greeted Rick when he answered.

"Missing Boy Scout. Apparently he wandered off the trail during a sunrise hike. The scoutmaster followed the usual procedures, but no sign of him."

I glanced at my watch. Almost noon. "Damn," I said. Why did everyone wait so long to ask for help? "Where-abouts?"

"We need you to search Catbird Ridge. We're assembling at the trailhead now. How long will it take you?"

"Twenty minutes." With the cordless phone in hand, I was already on my way to the house to gather up my gear. "I'll meet you at the trailhead and work down."

"We're having supplies brought for a night search if we need them."

"Let's hope we don't."

I clicked off and flung open the back door, grabbing my pack and a jacket from the hook in the mudroom, scraping off my shoes and stuffing my feet into the hiking boots that stood ready by the door. I opened my mouth to call, "Cisco!" but he was already there, claws skidding on the slick linoleum as he came to a stop before me, panting and grinning excitedly. He knew the routine.

I knotted my laces and snatched his orange search and rescue vest from the hook. "Cisco, dress," I told him, and he stood still, lowering his head as I slipped the vest over it and buckled it around his chest. "Okay, bud, let's go to work."

I scrawled a note to Maude and tacked it on the kennel door, and Cisco and I were halfway up the mountain before another five minutes passed.

Chapter Seven

At least ninety percent of my search and rescue work involves tourists who come to the mountains for a taste of nature and find that, in nature, they have bitten off more than they can chew. A surprising number of these are so-called wilderness experts—which is precisely why the forest service likes to keep a particularly close eye on the wilderness camping areas. The Nantahala Forest is one of the densest, most complex natural regions in the country; cell phones don't work here; helicopters can't land here; gorges, rivers and sheer rock faces can turn an afternoon hike into a life-or-death ordeal for the inexperienced. The average American is so accustomed to being entertained, taken care of and made comfortable that he honestly doesn't realize that there are still some places in this world where the dangers are real, the isolation is complete and there's no one to sue if he gets hurt.

For the ordinary dumb tourist camper, it's easy to forget he's not in Disneyland, and that no matter how far away from camp he strays he will not eventually come upon a sign with a map saying YOU ARE HERE. So he will wander for days, cold, dehydrated and disoriented, until he eventually succumbs to exposure or injury.

The more experienced wilderness camper, on the other hand, is just as often a victim of his own cockiness. He spies an interesting botanical specimen or animal track only a few dozen yards off the trail, or he is deceived by what sounds like the babbling of a nearby brook, only to discover that the brook was in fact much farther away than he had thought. When he turns to retrace his steps, there are no steps to retrace and no sign whatsoever of the trail he has just left.

The wilderness expert, however, does have a few small advantages over the dumb tourist when both are lost in the woods: He has at least a rudimentary knowledge of survival skills, and he knows enough—hopefully—not to keep moving once he realizes he is lost. A Boy Scout, in particular, should be trained to find a sheltered spot and stay there, intermittently blowing a whistle or using some other noisemaker, until he is found.

Unfortunately what is happening more and more these days is that young people are so ingrained with the concept of "stranger danger" that they will actually refuse to answer the calls of rescuers who are searching for them. Over and over stories are told of rescue teams coming within yards of a lost child who was huddling in the bushes, too afraid to call out for help.

That's where the SAR dogs come in.

I am not the only member of the Mountain Search and Rescue organization; just the closest to the actual wilderness where most of the need occurs, so I am usually the first one called. In the case of a missing child, especially with less than six hours left before dark, I knew that teams from neighboring counties had already been called. I only hoped we would find the boy before they got here.

I'm happy to say that most of these situations turn out for the good. Very often by the time we form the search party, the missing camper will stagger back, sweaty and scared but otherwise unharmed. Sometimes he'll be lucky enough to catch a stray cell phone signal and call 911. Sometimes he'll hear us calling. Sometimes the dog will gallop right to him—case closed and everyone is home before supper. Those are the stories that don't make the paper. Those are the stories in which we professionals get to roll our eyes at each other in a silent commentary on "damn tourists," then clap each other on the shoulder and head on back home. Those are the stories I like.

But when you start out, you never know what kind of story it's going to end up being.

From the harried scoutmaster and his hoard of eager scout assistants, all of whom seemed to think this was the best part of the whole trip, we learned that Ryan Marcus, age ten, was a bright student, had multiple merit badges, and was fully aware of scout procedure when one became separated from the group. He was also, it turned out, an independent thinker who had taken off on his own to gather wild blueberries for breakfast. Cocky.

Proper procedure for SAR is to work in teams of two. In a case like this, though, with time of the essence and resources at a minimum, a dog and handler can count as a team of two. I liked it better that way. Cisco is young and, as much as I hate to admit it, still easily distracted. The less he has to contend with, the better chance of success we have.

We started down the leaf-strewn trail with Cisco on a fifteen-foot cotton lead, nose to the ground and tail wagging happily, occasionally bounding off the trail and back again, halting, doubling back, circling and charging forward; looking for all the world like he knew exactly what he was doing. Of course the secret to making yourself look like a genius dog trainer is to find out what your dog loves and keep reinforcing him for doing it. Cisco loves to track. Sometimes I am not sure that he knows the difference between a cotton glove, a human victim and a family of bunnies quivering under a rock; he only knows that when he finds it, there is a party. So with great joy and anticipation of the hunt, Cisco set out to find whatever there was to be found.

And, approximately forty-five minutes later, he did exactly that.

By this time we had long passed the point of the original Boy Scout sunrise hike and were approaching a steep, narrow section that was clearly marked ADVANCED HIKERS ONLY on the map. Below the trail, however, was a crisscross of overgrown logging roads that eventually gave way to a seldom-used dirt road that circled around, after fifteen or twenty miles, toward the lake. I held out a vague hope that a smart little Boy Scout might actually have tried to seek out civilization by following the road. I really, really hoped he had not stayed on the trail, which became more treacherous the higher it climbed.

I felt a shaft of relief and cautious encouragement
when Cisco abruptly veered off the trail and through the
woods toward the logging roads. I followed him at a
clumsy jog, trying to keep his line from getting tangled
in the undergrowth. At this point I usually unleashed
Cisco, but to be honest, I wanted to make sure he wasn't
tracking a deer or a raccoon before I let him go. I had
spent too many exhausting hours chasing my otherwise
reliable dog through the woods to trust him entirely.

Fifteen feet ahead of me Cisco paused, excitedly
sniffed the ground and bounded off down the logging
road, all but dragging me behind him. *Deer,* I thought in
dismay, for he was far too sure of himself to be on the
track of anything useful. *Great.* I opened my mouth to
call him back. But just then Cisco skidded to a stop, sat
down abruptly and gave a single startled bark.

I should point out that this behavior is Cisco's "alert";
it means he has found what he was looking for. In this
case the bark did not sound triumphant; it was not the
bark of a dog who had done his job and was eager for his
reward. It sounded surprised, confused and a little disappointed. No wonder. Cisco had not bravely tracked his
victim through thicket and bramble only to find him
helpless but grateful in a leaf-covered ditch—which is
how we practiced in tracking class. He had, in fact, practically bumped into his target as the Boy Scout came
strolling around a bend in the road, drinking a Coke and
munching on a giant-sized bag of potato chips.

I stared at him. "Hey," I said.

"Hey," he replied, looking far less surprised to see me
than I was to see him.

"Are you Ryan?"

"Yeah." He glanced at Cisco. "Is that your dog?"

A little belatedly, I remembered my training and dug quickly into my backpack for the knotted rope toy that was Cisco's reward for a good find. "Good boy, Cisco, good find," I told him and tossed the toy. He caught it in midair, gave it a few happy shakes and then dropped it on the ground, looking expectantly at Ryan—or rather, at the bag of chips.

I said, "Cisco is a search and rescue dog. He's been looking for you."

"No kidding." He looked moderately impressed and munched a handful of chips. "Well, here I am."

I took out my walkie-talkie and spoke into it. "Base, this is K-9 One," I said. "We have him. He's ambulatory and appears unharmed."

Rick's voice crackled back, "Where are you?"

I said, glancing around, "About half a mile from Hawkins Mill, on the north ridge logging road. If you send a jeep we wouldn't object to a ride back."

"On our way. Good work, Raine. Tell Cisco I've got a dog biscuit with his name on it."

"I'm afraid you're going to have to do better than dog biscuits to compete with what he's got his eye on now. K-9 One out.

"A lot of people have been looking for you," I told Ryan, tucking the radio back into my pack. "Your scoutmaster was very worried."

"Does your dog like chips?" Ryan asked.

"No," I lied, although it was hard to sound convincing while Cisco was licking long strings of drool from his lips and gazing at the bag of chips with all the yearning of a lost soul for the pearly gates.

Ryan tossed Cisco a potato chip and Cisco caught it in midair with a satisfied crunch. Ryan laughed and I said, "Please don't feed my dog."

"He likes them," insisted the little smart aleck and dug in the bag for more.

"He's allergic," I told him, which gave him pause. And then it occurred to me that no one had mentioned that the sunrise hikers had been outfitted with drinks and giant bags of chips. As I looked closely I saw that the pockets of his uniform were bulging with what appeared to be chocolate cookies. "Where did you get those, anyway?"

A wary look came over his face. "It wasn't really stealing. The car was empty, and the door was open. I called and looked around, but no one came. Besides, the first rule of survival is to find food and shelter. I should get a merit badge."

I wanted to tell him that the first rule of survival was not to get yourself lost in the first place, but about half a beat behind his words, I actually heard what they meant.

I said, looking at him closely, "What car? Where?"

He gestured back down the road. "Down there, off in the woods. There were lots of groceries and stuff inside, but looks like squirrels and possums already got most of it. I drank most of the Cokes," he added. "My dad will pay."

I said, hardly daring to think what I was thinking, "Is it very far? Do you think you could show me where it is?"

He shrugged. "Sure." He tossed Cisco another chip and turned back down the road. "Say, do you think I'll get my picture in the paper?"

"I wouldn't be a bit surprised," I murmured, and gathered up Cisco's leash. "Come on, boy, let's go."

Less than an hour later, I was perched on the open tailgate of a forest service vehicle, stroking Cisco's fur while he enjoyed the dog biscuit Rick had promised him, watching as sheriff's deputies roped off the area surrounding a silver PT Cruiser at the bottom of a small gorge. The path the car had taken when it left the dirt road was easy to see—downed saplings and crushed shrubs marked a swath. However, the car had managed to bury itself in the foliage of an uprooted hemlock when it came to rest, and it might have been months before a vehicle passing on this seldom-used dirt road spotted it.

Ryan Marcus, boy of the hour, was on his way back to base camp in a forest service Jeep, where he would be welcomed as a hero, have his picture taken for the paper and be bundled home to his mummy and daddy. There he would be showered with all the chips he could eat and soda he could drink. This was one of the good stories.

So far.

Buck made his way back up the slope to me, a task made slightly more difficult by the fact that the path of least resistance—the one the car had left on its way down—was now bracketed on either side by yellow crime scene tape. He lifted his hat when he reached me and wiped his forehead with the back of his sleeve.

"The registration papers say the car belongs to

Michelle White," he told me. Resting an arm on the car roof, he leaned down to ruffle Cisco's neck fur. "Good job, boy."

Cisco grinned up at him.

"Keys were in the ignition," he said, and nodded toward the path the car had taken when it left the road. "Looks like the driver tried to take the curve too fast and plowed right off into the woods."

"That would be easy to do at night," I observed.

He shrugged. "Or if the driver was drunk, or swerving to miss a deer, or just not paying attention."

I guess that's why they paid him the deputy money. He never went for the obvious answer just because it was easy.

"The air bag deployed when the car hit the tree," Buck went on. "So far no clue about the driver." He glanced at Cisco. "I don't suppose . . ."

I shook my head. Aside from the fact that I *hate* doing police work—the last time Cisco and I had assisted in a police search I had stumbled over a body with its face blown off and I still wasn't over that one—this was an easy call. "The kid's scent is all over the car and all around it. Cisco's not discriminating enough yet to ignore that find and understand that he's supposed to go after another one. It would just be a waste of time. You're better off waiting for Hank to get here with the bloodhounds."

Hank Baker was my team leader and the real expert when it came to search and rescue. The fact that he lived two hours away, however, meant that the best I could do when things got complicated was to try not to contaminate the trail too much before he arrived.

Buck nodded, squinting back down the slope. "We popped the trunk," he said. "There are a couple suitcases, a wheelchair and a service dog harness. We're not going to move anything until the state crime lab van gets here, but it looks like enough luggage for a couple of weeks, maybe more. The backseat is full of groceries—dry goods mostly, cereal, coffee, paper towels, sodas; the kind of things people bring with them to a vacation house. The bags were from a Publix outside of Mount Pleasant. What the kid didn't eat, the varmints got to. Looks like a chipmunk's picnic in the backseat."

"No dog food?"

He shook his head. "Not even an empty bag."

"So when Jeff didn't have the brand he was looking for, he must have decided to go someplace else for it."

"Where else is there?"

I shrugged. "No place around here. But lots of places in Asheville."

Buck looked skeptical. "Come on, honey, that's over an hour away. Who drives that far on a vacation for dog food?"

I said simply, "Someone whose life depends on their dog."

He didn't look convinced. "This is not exactly on the way to Asheville."

I said, "Right. You'd have to be pretty lost to end up this far off the highway looking for a pet store."

"Or pretty scared."

I lifted an eyebrow questioningly.

"You're thinking dog food, I'm thinking homicide," Buck said. "A guy who has just killed his wife is a lot more likely to run his car off a dirt road in the middle of nowhere than a guy who is on his way to Asheville for dog food."

I was about to point out the flaw in this logic when there was a shout from below. Buck turned and I hopped to the ground, moving for a better look at the activity down below. Cisco followed, tail held high and waving. He barked a greeting to two of the familiar faces who, after another moment, started up the hill toward us, a leather satchel held in careful balance between them. As they grew closer, I could tell they were struggling under the weight, trying not to let the satchel hit the ground. Buck scrambled down the slope to help them up the last few yards.

"What's the deal?" I heard him say. "I thought we weren't moving anything until the crime techs had a go at it."

"Sheriff's orders," said one of the deputies, breathing hard as they reached flat ground. "Said we ought to secure this in a patrol car until the van gets here."

"What's in it?" Buck asked.

Instinctively I slipped my hand through Cisco's collar and took a few steps backward as I had an awful thought about what—or who—might be in the satchel. Too many gruesome crime movies, I guess.

Without another word, one of the deputies flipped the latch on the bag, and the two men spread it open between them by the handles. I couldn't help myself. I looked.

The bag was filled with gold coins.

Chapter Eight

"Well, quite a day's work, all in all, I would say," remarked Maude, lifting her teacup to me in a small salute. "You resolved the identity of a dead woman, opened a homicide investigation, tracked down the rightful owners of a valuable service dog, found a lost Boy Scout and discovered a bag full of treasure. Nicely done. Nicely done indeed."

"Not to mention cussing out my new neighbor and alienating one of the richest men in the Southeast," I pointed out. I sat back in my chair and swung my feet up onto the battered hassock in front of it, affecting an attitude of smugness. "Not bad at all."

Maude still likes to take an afternoon tea break, although during the busy time of the year she doesn't often get to do it. I prefer cocoa, myself, and even though I still had several hours worth of work waiting for me in the kennel, I felt I deserved a celebratory cup. We had a fire going in the fireplace, the dogs were sprawled out in their various favorite places and even

Hero had been persuaded to leave his crate and come lie beside my chair. Cisco, who was gnawing on a hard rubber bone on the other side of my chair, was the picture of contentment. At four thirty in the afternoon the sun had already begun to drop behind the mountain, and the room was bathed in a pleasant dusky glow. It was one of my favorite times of day.

I said, sipping the cocoa, "What kind of person keeps a bag of gold coins in his car, anyway? It's like something out of a fairy tale."

The police were not releasing the fact that a bag of coins had been found in the car trunk until the state investigators gave them clearance, but telling Maude was not the same as telling the media. Unless my uncle ordered me directly not to do so, I always felt free to discuss cases with Maude.

"I doubt very seriously whether he was accustomed to carrying around a bag of gold coins," Maude pointed out. "Obviously he, or she—let's not forget the car was registered in her name—intended to do something with them. And since gold is internationally negotiable, I suspect that what he intended to do was to leave the country."

"He sure picked an odd starting point. We aren't exactly next door to an international border."

"Perhaps he was on his way to the airport when the car crashed. Asheville has international flights, and the logic might well be that security would be less intense at a smaller airport."

"Makes sense I guess," I agreed. "Of course, you'd have to connect through Atlanta to go anywhere, but if you checked your baggage through to your final destination you might have less trouble getting through security in Asheville."

"Certainly the wait time is less, if time was a consideration."

"True enough."

I reached down absently to scratch Hero's ears, and Cisco looked up alertly.

"Is the theory that the poor man is injured or dead?"

"They didn't find any blood in the car," I said. "But I can't think of any other reason why a man would walk off and leave a bag full of gold coins. He may have tried to hike back to the road and gotten lost. After all, if a Boy Scout can get turned around just a few yards off the trail, a city slicker from Charleston wouldn't have much of a chance. Hank and the bloodhounds will be out looking first thing in the morning."

"I'd like to know what he was doing out there in the first place. That old road isn't easy to find."

"Well, if we knew that, I guess a lot of questions would be answered."

Maude frequently brings me homemade goodies. My favorite are her blueberry scones, but running a close second are the tea cakes that were arranged on a china plate with a paper doily and set on an end table carefully out of reach of curious dog noses. Cisco watched intensely as I reached for one, and didn't stop watching until I had consumed every morsel.

"There's still a lot about this that doesn't add up, though," I said. "I wish your friend Letty would call back. It sounded as though she knew the Whites personally. I'll bet she could answer a lot of questions." I had told Maude about the overseas phone call she had missed, and I had also told Uncle Roe that Letty Cranston could be found in Crete. Of course the fact that she had lost the connection before leaving a return phone number did not make her any easier to track down.

"Oh, bloody hell," Maude said abruptly, and I looked at her in surprise. "Speaking of missed phone calls, in all the excitement I completely forgot. That fellow from Coastal Assistance Dogs returned your call. I told him about the incident this morning with the gunfire, and he seemed most concerned. He wanted to talk to you personally. He said he'd be in the office until five."

I hurried to find the number and place the call.

It was put through immediately, and Wes sounded relieved to hear from me. We talked for a few moments about the jumping-through-the-window episode, and I assured him that there was no serious physical injury. But I knew that his concerns about the dog went beyond the Lab's physical well-being.

"I'm sure I don't have to tell you that this kind of behavior is deeply alarming," he told me. "Even a one-time occurrence can make the dog too unreliable to be returned to service."

My heart sank. My instinct was to make excuses for Hero—he had just been through a terrible trauma, he was stressed both physically and mentally and if this had never happened before, surely he deserved a second chance. But by force of will I kept my mouth shut. This man was the expert, not I. And people's lives really were at stake.

I said, "If you can't take him back into the program, what will happen to him?"

"Oh, we have a list of highly qualified applicants waiting to adopt one of our retired service dogs," he assured me. "Very often they can be placed as a pet with a member of the deceased's family." He hesitated. "But in this case I see there is only the husband and a father."

I said, "The husband still hasn't been located." And because I thought, on behalf of Hero, he had the right to know, I added, "There's a possibility he might not be, um, able to care for a dog." This was true, whether he was found injured, dead or guilty of murder. I could sense the puzzlement in Wes's silence but didn't feel free to elaborate.

He said, "I found a volunteer who can pick Nero up on Saturday, but I could arrange to be in your area later next week. I'll be driving back from Atlanta. I'd like to evaluate Nero myself, and then I could bring him back with me. I know it's an imposition to ask you to keep him—"

"Not at all," I assured him. "He's really no trouble. I like having him around. And now that I know about his noise phobia, I'll definitely keep him closer to me. I got your fax of his list of commands, and I can keep practicing with him. Do you think it would be okay to take him out in public some?"

"That would probably be good for him," Wes said. "Just be sure he minds his manners, and don't let him get away with anything a service dog shouldn't be doing."

"I don't think that will be problem," I said, looking across the room at those sweet liquid eyes gazing at me from the floor.

"I can't tell you how much I appreciate this, Miss Stockton. I'll be in touch."

Maude was clearing away the tea things as I returned. "I take it we have a boarder for a little while longer?"

I nodded, snatching another tea cake before she removed the plate. "He wants to come down and get the dog himself next week. That's fine with me. I always wanted to train a service dog. I mean, I know that's not what I'm actually doing, but just taking him through his paces is fascinating to me."

Maude cast a skeptical glance in the direction of Hero, who had not once moved from the place I had assigned him on the floor by my chair. "I don't know, my dear. He still doesn't look like he's quite up to being put through any paces."

"His heart may not be in it, but he's too well trained not carry out his commands. Watch this."

I snatched one of the napkins from the tray Maude was carrying and dropped it on the floor. "Hero," I said. "Take." I pointed to the napkin.

The Lab pushed to his feet, ambled over to the napkin, picked it up off the floor and returned to sit in front of me. "Good," I told him, and held out my hand. "Drop."

He released the slightly soggy napkin into my hand. I praised him and ruffled his ears. He seemed to tolerate, rather than appreciate, my affection.

Maude said, "Very nice. Now if he would just do the dishes and tidy the kitchen before he goes to bed, we'd be all set, wouldn't we?"

"Well, I don't know about the dishes, but he can at least lock up and turn off the lights for us. Hero, door."

Hero trotted toward the front door, jumped up and clawed at the doorknob until he turned the deadbolt and it locked into place. I clapped my hands and exclaimed, "Good boy! Now, lights."

For a moment he was confused, since he had only recently learned where the light switch was in this house. Then he located the white switch plate on the wall by the door, leapt up and pawed the switch off. The two table lamps that were controlled by the switch went off and the room was left in dimness. I exclaimed again, "Wonderful! Good boy, Hero!"

Cisco, alerted by the enthusiasm in my voice, got up and looked around expectantly for the treat that usually accompanied that level of vocal enthusiasm. In his mind, all things good in the universe centered around him.

"Very clever," agreed Maude, still holding the tray. "I don't suppose he could, er . . ." She gestured to the light switch with one shoulder.

Heady with my own power, I said, "Hero, lights."

Hero jumped up and pawed the light switch again.

A golden blur charged across my peripheral vision, accompanied by a snarling, sharp-voiced bark that was so outrageous coming from my mild-mannered golden retriever that at first I didn't recognize it. Cisco leapt on Hero and knocked him to the ground, and the whole world erupted into a confusion of rolling yellow dog bodies and furious vocalizations. Majesty sprang to her feet and started barking; the two Aussies charged forward, excitedly cheering the combatants on; the tea tray clattered as Maude set it aside and moved quickly to grab the collars of the nearest dogs.

It was over in a matter of seconds. The Lab yelped and Cisco gave a final series of hell-houndish vocalizations. I shouted, "Cisco, leave!" and the moment he turned his head I grabbed his collar and marched him silently out of the house and into the backyard, where I exiled him behind a locked dog door.

By the time I returned, Maude had my other three dogs in their crates—a testament to her efficiency and smooth handling skills—and Hero was cowering under a table.

"Damn," I said. My heart was thundering in my chest. "Damn, damn, damn. Is he hurt?"

"Not even a speck of slobber on him," replied Maude mildly. "It was all talk."

But whether he was injured or not, I knew the kind of psychological damage that could be done to a dog who has been attacked by another dog. Something like this could turn a formerly social dog into an aggressor, or trigger a fear of others of its own kind that could last a lifetime. As if the poor thing hadn't been through enough. The fact that *my* dog had been the aggressor . . . My Cisco who had actually attacked a service dog who was performing his duties . . . I could hardly get my mind around that. I just couldn't believe what I had seen.

"What in the world got into him?" I demanded shakily. I sank to the floor beside the table where the Lab was hiding and dug into my pocket for treats. "I've never seen anything like that in my life. Cisco isn't aggressive! What happened?" I realized that I sounded like half the clients who came to me wanting me to "fix" their aggressive dogs. The one thing they all had in common was denial. But this was Cisco!

"Calm down," Maude said in that same easy, matter-of-fact tone she used to calm spooked animals. "You're not doing this fellow any favors by shoving cheese into his face. Leave him be."

She was right, of course. My body language radiated tension, and I was crowding a dog who already felt trapped. I left a few tidbits on the floor and moved away several feet, consciously trying to relax my shoulders.

"He's jealous, that's what it is," I said. I deliberately forced my voice into a close approximation of Maude's calm tone. "I've been paying too much attention to Hero, and this is Cisco's way of trying to eliminate the competition."

"Dogs don't have secondary emotions," Maude reminded me. "More likely, he saw Hero's jumping behavior as a threat, and he was defending himself—or you."

I knew her explanation was the most logical one, and I wanted to believe it. But it's hard not to anthropomorphize when your dog does something as shocking and as completely out of character as Cisco had just done.

Maude said, "Hero, here."

Hero left the shelter of the table and came to her, his tail low but wagging. She stroked his ear. "Let Cisco in on a lead. Likely he's completely forgotten the whole thing by now."

I did as she requested, and of course she was right. The two dogs sniffed noses, wagged tails and lost interest. Hero went to his crate, and Cisco looked up at me as though wondering why he was on a leash inside the house.

"Just watch them for a while," Maude advised. She unsnapped Cisco's lead and he went back to his rubber bone. "They'll be fine."

But for the first time I began to feel as though five dogs inside the house might be too many.

Chapter Nine

After that unsettling incident I was supersensitive to the possibility of another, and when I was awakened by the sound of violent barking before daylight the next morning, I shot out of bed and was halfway down the stairs before I realized that the noise couldn't possibly herald another dogfight: All the dogs were crated except Cisco, and he was right on my heels. I made my way groggily down the remainder of the stairs, quieting the dogs with a sharp word. Of course, quieting a herding dog is more easily said than done, and since most of the barking was coming from the two Aussies and the collie, all I got was an occasional break in the chorus.

In the spates of silence I was able to discern what had set them off in the first place—the grinding sound of heavy-equipment engines as they rounded the curve in the road at the end of my drive. Standing on tiptoe to look out the high glass window in the front door, I could see the flash of headlights from the highway—two, three, four big trucks lumbered their way up a grade that rarely saw more than a dozen vehicles of any description each day. Who in the world would be transporting heavy equipment along this little-used road at five forty-five in the morning?

It took even my foggy brain only a moment to make the connection. *Tomorrow we bring in the bulldozers.*

"Thank you very much, Mr. Miles Young," I muttered. Was this what I had to look forward to all winter?

The barks quieted down as the last truck whined its way into the distance, and the dogs stood alertly in their crates, anticipating, in the way only dogs can at five forty-five in the morning, another wonderful and exciting day. I checked first on Hero, who, in perfect service dog fashion, had not barked but simply stood, edged toward the back of his crate, awaiting whatever I required of him. He did not seem particularly distressed by either the loud trucks or Cisco's presence, but he was far from exhibiting the happy insouciance of the Aussies or the grinning, tail-curling stretches of the collie. I let Cisco and the other three dogs out into the yard; then I came back for Hero. Maude was probably right—the disagreement (I couldn't bring myself to call it a fight) had been a one-time incident that was by now completely forgotten by both dogs. But I did not want to risk another one.

Though I cursed Miles Young for every lost second of sleep, the advantage of having been awakened before dawn was that I had a head start on the day. I finished feeding and exercising the kennel dogs, cleaned the runs, laundered the dog beds, sterilized the dog dishes and brought the accounts up to date. Since it was still too early to make or return phone calls, I spent some time working with Hero.

It broke my heart to think that such an incredible dog might never again do the work for which he was trained. And even though I knew, intellectually, that once the temperament of a service dog broke down there was very little that could be done to correct it, I was determined to do what I could to prepare him to shine in the eyes of Wes Richards when he arrived to evaluate him next week.

I locked Cisco in the office while I worked with Hero in the training room, and I could hear him barking indignantly. When it came to treats, or the possibility of treats, he had extrasensory perception.

Although nothing about Hero's demeanor demonstrated enthusiasm for his work, and though he often showed such reluctance to obey as to require an admonishment, it was an unmitigated thrill for me to work with a dog who could perform complex tasks on command. I was amazed to the point of delighted laughter on more than one occasion and felt a brief stab of jealousy for those lucky trainers who actually got to work with dogs of this caliber every day.

A little after eight, the phone rang. I had brought the portable phone with me to the training room and left it on the sign-in table by the door. I knew from the list that Wes had faxed me that Hero was supposed to be able to take the phone in his mouth and bring it on command, whether or not it was ringing. So I told him, "Phone," and even though it was cheating, I pointed him toward the place where the portable phone chirruped on the table.

His response time was so slow that if I hadn't met him halfway across the room the caller surely would have hung up before Hero brought me the phone. But it was such a wonderful thing to see the Lab cross the room, put his paws up on the table, take the phone in his mouth and start to return to me with it that I called the exercise a success. I offered him a treat as I pushed the TALK button, but Hero simply turned away, crossed the room to an empty crate and lay down inside it.

"Mornin', sweetie," Buck said when he heard my voice.

"Guess who just answered the phone?" I demanded happily.

"Ummm, wait, don't tell me. . . . You?"

"Wrong. Hero."

"The dog?"

"That's right."

"He didn't have much to say."

"Very funny. He can turn lights on and off and lock and unlock doors too."

"Good for him."

"Don't tell me you don't find that impressive."

"Not as much as you do. I can't say I've ever met a service dog groupie before. Now, that's impressive."

"You're just full of them today, aren't you? What do you want?"

"Bad news, looks like. Or maybe good news, depending on how you look at it."

"You found the husband?"

"I'm afraid so. The dogs picked up the trail just before dawn. He was found facedown in the stream about half a mile from the car. Looks like he knocked himself out on a rock and drowned before he regained consciousness. They think he's been dead a couple of days at least."

"Wow," I said somberly. I didn't know what else to say. "Drowned."

"Yeah."

"What about the bag full of gold?"

"As in, what was he doing with it and why would he leave it? No idea. Mickey White's father is coming in this afternoon to claim her body. Maybe he can shed some light."

"This whole thing is just bizarre, if you ask me."

"Or me." His tone changed as he went on, "Anyway, the upshot is that I have the afternoon off. You want to do something?"

"Like what?"

"I don't know. Take Cisco to the lake or something?"

I said, "Cisco is not exactly on my A-list today." And before he could ask why I said, "But I can't. I promised Dolly I would pick up some folding tables and stuff that Sonny is loaning us and take them downtown so they'll be ready to set up Saturday morning."

"You need any help?"

"I could use the loan of your truck."

He said, "I might as well hang around the office and catch up on some paperwork, then. Tell you what. Why don't you come on by and pick up the truck whenever you're ready, and when you get back we'll go get something to eat."

"Sounds good to me. I don't think I can get away from here before two, though."

"I'll see you then."

When I returned to the office with gentle Hero on a lead by my side, Cisco was lying in the middle of the floor with his head between his paws, surrounded by shredded papers and the foam stuffing of an eviscerated sofa cushion. He had knocked over a display of leashes and turned over a plastic bin of training clickers, which were now scattered all over the floor. Maude, who had apparently come in moments before I had, stood at the door with folded arms, waiting for me to explode.

Of course we both knew it was pointless to scold a dog after the fact, and even at the height of temper I was able to remember that. Silently, I handed her Hero's leash, and I opened the door that led to the kennel yard. "Cisco, let's go," I said, and Cisco left the room for the play yard with tail wagging.

To Maude I said darkly, "Jealous."

And Maude replied, "Bored."

There is an adage: A dog is only as good as his trainer. And Cisco was making me look very, very bad. Yes, of course he was bored. And of course, anyone who left a two-year-old golden retriever unsupervised in a room full of breakables and shreddables deserved what she got. Nonetheless, Cisco's chances of going to the lake— ever—had just flown out the window, and I was now seriously reconsidering taking him to the Pet Fair this weekend, despite the fact that he was supposed to be one of the star attractions.

Cleaning up the damage put me behind schedule, and I forgot to call Sonny until I had already picked up the keys to Buck's truck and was on my way up the mountain toward her place. I tried my cell phone but couldn't get a signal. I could only hope that she hadn't forgotten I was coming.

Sonny had purchased a beautiful mountaintop spread a little over a year ago with the plan of turning it into a sanctuary for unwanted animals. Bit by bit she was restoring the corrals, stables and sheds that had come with the place in hopes of making them a suitable habitat for domestic and farm animals. So far she had a handful of sheep, a couple of goats with an attitude problem, a lame rooster, a donkey with a missing ear and, at last count, four cats who had apparently heard about the plans for a heated kitty condo and had made their way up the mountain to stake a claim before winter set in. The good thing about the remote location of Sonny's place was that people weren't inclined to stop by after dark and dump off boxes full of unwanted kittens and puppies, as they often did when they heard about a kindhearted animal lover in the country.

Naturally, when Dolly heard about Sonny's altrusistic instincts—not to mention her propensity for doing pro bono work—she pounced on her like, well, a cat on a mouse. The last I heard, Sonny not only had donated cash and goods to the upcoming Pet Fair, but was also dividing her time over the weekend between working the

Save the Mountains booth and manning the animal shelter booth.

And some people worry, when they move to a small mountain community, that they won't have anything to do.

The drive up to Sonny's house was gorgeous, if somewhat treacherous—a steep, twisting, rutted path canopied with golden poplars and bright red sweet gum trees. Sheer drop-offs on either side opened up an endless vista of layered mountains glowing yellow, orange, red and, in the deep distance, brilliant lavender. I had to continually remind myself to keep my eyes on the road—what there was of it.

I could hear Mystery barking as I got out of the car, and I caught a glimpse of her black-and-white face as she bounced up on the front window, then raced away—presumably to greet me at the door. One of the goats wandered toward the edge of its enclosure to see whether I had brought a carrot or anything else interesting, and the donkey brayed from the stable at the bottom of the hill. All else was quiet. As I climbed the front steps I noticed that the garage door was open, and Sonny's car was parked there. At least I hadn't made the trip all the way out here only to miss her.

I called, "Yoo-hoo!" and tapped on the glass-paned front door. Mystery flung herself against the panes, barking and clawing.

Usually by the time I reached the door, Sonny had it open, waiting to greet me. After all, there was not much chance of a visitor catching her by surprise with Mystery around. "Hey," I called over the sound of barking. "It's me!"

Mystery flung herself against the door so hard that the glass rattled, and I gave her a sharp, admonishing, "Mystery! Cut that out. Off!"

I don't like to correct someone else's dog, but I was, after all, Mystery's obedience instructor—one of them, anyway. Most of the time, she made me feel as though I was a pretty good teacher, but today, apparently, was not my day for self-congratulations in the well-behaved-dog department.

My sharp tone seemed to serve only to increase Mystery's bad behavior. Her barking had a frantic, almost crazed edge to it, and she wasn't just jumping at the door; she was charging it, clawing it, as though she were determined to do as much damage as she could. That wasn't like Mystery. She knew me. By now she should be sitting down and waving her tail along the floor, her eyes fixed upon the pocket where she knew I kept the treats. And why was Sonny allowing this?

I called again, "Sonny?" I tried the door, and it was unlocked, as I knew it would be. No one locked their doors around here. "It's Raine. Okay if I come in?"

I opened the door, fully expecting to be clawed to death by an overly enthusiastic border collie in wild greeting mode. I had even begun the pivot that would show her my back and discourage her from jumping when I realized Mystery was no longer there. She had, in fact, raced away from me, across the stone foyer and into the wide expanse that led to the kitchen and family room. There she stood, barking wildly.

I said, "Mystery, quiet!" and called out, "Sonny! Are you here?"

Mystery dashed across the floor, grabbed the leg of my jeans, and tore at it. This was such complete un-Mystery-like behavior that I couldn't even get out an astonished yelp before she had flown away again, toenails digging for traction into the stone floor as she came to a stop at exactly the same place and started barking again.

Every Lassie show I had ever seen suddenly flashed through my mind and I rushed across the foyer, calling, "Sonny? Sonny, are you all right?"

I turned toward the kitchen, but Mystery, circling and barking, herded me to the great room. There, on the floor between the big leather sofa and the hearth, I found my friend, lying in a pool of her own blood.

Chapter Ten

"I'm fine, really," Sonny said, waving away my offer of another pillow to support her back. "Don't fuss."

She was sitting on the sofa with a butterfly bandage closing the cut on her forehead, a cashmere throw over her legs and Mystery curled up contentedly beside her. Her blood-spattered clothes had been changed for clean ones and she was sipping a cup of herbal tea. All in all she looked as though she was doing much better than I was.

I said, "You should have let the paramedics take you to the hospital." I sank into the chair next to her, trying not to sound as anxious as I felt. "After all, they came all this way."

She made a face. "Thank you very much, but I prefer not to spend the next six hours in an emergency room just so some doctor I've never met can prescribe aspirin and rest and tell me to see my own physician in the morning. I have aspirin here and an appointment with Dr. George Shepler at eleven a.m."

It had taken the paramedics almost an hour to get here, and by that time Sonny was just as calm and in control as she was now. She added, not for the first time, "It was just a stupid accident. My leg gave out, and I hit my head on the coffee table. Head cuts make such a mess. It looked a lot worse than it was. I'll wake up black-and-blue in the morning, but not much the worse for wear."

I said, seriously, "You need to get the road to the house paved. You saw how long it took the ambulance to get here. In the winter they might not be able to make it at all."

She met my eyes, and I saw a flash of anger there, a struggle with defiance she was trying hard not to voice. I knew what her independence meant to her, and living on the top of a mountain at the end of an almost impassable trail was an extra declaration of self-reliance of which she was particularly proud.

But Sonny was no fool, either. She had remodeled the house to make it wheelchair friendly, and she used the chair without embarrassment or reluctance when she had to. She knew her limitations and was prepared for them.

She sighed. "You're right. I should have taken care of that this summer. It's just that I've been feeling so well. It's silly, I know. This is not a condition that gets better. But for a while there I forgot that. I even started thinking about doing things I never would have considered before—like entering Mystery in some herding trials next spring. Poor thing." She stroked the border collie's shapely head. "It hardly seems fair to her."

I said sternly, "Don't be ridiculous. You know perfectly well that the dog does all the work in a herding trial, and there's nothing in this world stopping you from handling her from a chair. If you want to put her in a trial, I'll make sure you get the premium as soon as it's printed."

She returned a distant smile. "We'll see." She took another sip of her tea, holding the cup with both hands. "It's just so depressing, knowing it's all downhill from here. Hard to think about spring."

I thought about Mickey White, who had been almost completely confined to a wheelchair, and whose prognosis was much worse than Sonny's. I said, "Now I know you need to go have that head injury checked out. Self-pity is definitely not like you. There must be something wrong."

She made a wry face. "You're right. I should be ashamed of myself." She rested her hand on Mystery's silky neck. "I think I scared her half to death. She tried to help, she just didn't know what to do."

"She did fine," I assured Sonny. "You should have seen her trying to lead me to you, just like one of those dogs in the movies."

I hesitated, but I had to say it. "Sonny . . . have you ever thought about having somebody move in up here? I mean, with it being so far off the beaten track and everything, it might be good to have somebody to, you know, keep an eye on"—I almost said "you" but made a quick substitution—"things. A housekeeper, or a caretaker. Maybe even a couple."

Her cool, steady gaze told me that she knew exactly what I was trying to suggest—that she hire a nurse—and precisely how she felt about that idea.

With a deliberate change of subject, Sonny said, "I heard about you and Cisco on the radio yesterday. Quite an adventure."

Relieved for the opportunity to talk about less sensitive subjects, I brought her up to date on the Mickey White case, including the discovery of the body of Leo White this morning, drowned in the creek.

"Good heavens," she said, "this story just keeps getting stranger. How is Hero taking it all?"

I sighed. "He still seems depressed. And Cisco isn't helping any." Briefly, I related the incident between Hero and Cisco that had occurred the night before.

"Well, you can hardly blame him," Sonny said. "After all, up until now there's only been one hero in the family—him. And he *did* find that Boy Scout yesterday. Maybe you should have made a bigger fuss."

I chuckled. "Actually, I think the Boy Scout found us."

"Maybe Cisco would like to learn how to do some of the things Hero knows," suggested Sonny. "At the very least, I think he'd enjoy the extra attention he'd get from the training."

"That's a good idea," I said, surprised that I hadn't thought of it myself. "He'd probably be a natural at some of those behaviors. After all, he is a retriever."

"I wouldn't be a bit surprised."

I said, "I think I'm going to bring Hero to the Pet Fair Saturday. It'll be good for him to be around noise and people, and I'd like to do as much socialization as possible with him before he's taken back for evaluation."

We talked in that vein for a while, and I let Sonny

guide the conversation toward topics that had nothing to do with her disability or the frightening accident that afternoon. By the time I felt comfortable enough to leave her—in fact, she practically forced me to leave—it was almost dark. I loaded up the supplies I had come for and started down the mountain.

There was no sign of either Buck or my car in the parking lot when I arrived back at the sheriff's department, but the lights were still on in my uncle's office. I tapped lightly on the frame of the open door and stuck my head inside.

"Hey," I said, holding up the keys to Buck's truck. "Was he very mad?"

Uncle Roe looked up from the computer screen over which he was hunched. "Hey, Rainbow. How's your friend?"

Naturally, they would have known about the 911 call, and probably had heard the radio transmission from the paramedics relaying that Sonny's injuries were minor. "Okay," I said. "It was just a scratch. But it was scary."

He nodded and stretched one arm across his chest to rub his shoulder. In the harsh fluorescent lights he looked tired, almost haggard. "That's what Ranelle heard on the scanner. Buck took your car. He said he'd meet you at home."

"Whose home?" For some reason, I still felt compelled to point out at every opportunity that Buck and I were not, in fact, living together. "Mine or his?"

He looked surprised that I would ask. "Didn't say."

I shrugged it away, embarrassed. "Never mind, stupid question." Then I said, "Are you okay? You look beat."

"Damn computers," he grumbled, "give me neck ache. Oh, say, that Mickey White's father was in here today." He rummaged in his desk drawer for something and came up with a card, which he held out to me. "Hell of a thing, having to tell a man he's lost his daughter and his son-in-law all in one week. But he was asking about the dog. I told him you were taking care of that, but he left his card for you, just in case. He wrote his cell phone number on back."

"Thanks." I took the card. "I'll call him. Did you get the message about Letty Cranston?"

He nodded. "We'll try to track down a phone number for her, but the main thing we wanted to know was the identity of the renters, so it's not really urgent."

"She sounded like she knew these people. She might be able to fill in the background."

"Speaking of background, guess who made a living buying and trading coins on the Internet?"

"Leo White?"

He nodded. "So it looks like the bag of gold might have been legitimate—assuming he was abiding by all the federal and tax rules governing that kind of thing. We're still looking into it."

"Maude thinks he might have been thinking about leaving the country."

"That'd be my guess."

"Which makes him look more and more guilty of pre-meditated murder."

"Afraid so."

I brushed my uncle's cheek with a kiss. "Go home and

get some supper. Really, you look awful. Take a break. The computer will be here in the morning."

He sighed. "Ain't that the truth?"

My car was, in fact, parked in its customary place when I returned home; the porch light was on and I could smell wood smoke coming from the chimney. I had to admit, it was a welcoming feeling to know that someone waited for me inside after the day I had had, that the dogs had been fed and supper was ready and all I had to do was to stretch out in front of the fire and relax.

When I opened the door, the air smelled like cinnamon and the room was awash in the golden glow of firelight and dozens of candles. They were on the mantel, on the end tables, on the hearth, on the bookshelves, on the floor. The first thing I said was, "Where are the dogs?"

"In their crates, where they belong." Buck, in silhouette, arose from tending the fire and came toward me. "It's past their bedtime, you know."

I shrugged out of my jacket. "Did the power go out?"

"You're such a romantic." Buck kissed me and pressed a glass of wine into my hand.

"Wine," I said, surprised. We usually drank beer.

Buck said, "How's Sonny?"

"It wasn't serious." I sipped the wine. "Nice," I complimented him. "Where's Cisco?" The other dogs might well be sleeping, but the only time Cisco remained quiet in a crate was in the car, and then only rarely.

"Being a good dog for a change." Buck took my hand and led me to the sofa, where Cisco was curled contentedly. He looked up at me and thumped his tail, but did not attempt to leave his perch.

"Now that's what I call self-confidence," I said. "Leaving a golden retriever in a 'down-stay' with all these candles around."

"We have an understanding, Cisco and I. He gets to stay here while we have supper as long as he doesn't set one paw off the sofa."

"You brought food too?"

"I made beef stew last night. It's warming on the stove."

Buck's mother had been one of the best cooks in Hanover County, and she was determined that none of her boys—there were three of them—was ever going to go hungry for lack of a woman to cook for him. Good thing too, because both Buck and I would have surely starved during our marriage if he had waited for me to cook.

"What smells like cinnamon?"

"Meg just made a fresh batch of apple pies this morning." Meg owned a popular eating establishment that was known for some of the best pies in the state. "I've got one keeping warm in the oven." He hesitated. "There might be a slice missing."

I laughed and let him pull me down to the cushions he had arranged in front of the fireplace. "This is nice, Buck." I lifted my glass. "The wine and all. Real nice."

He smiled, toying with my fingers. "Yeah, it is, isn't it? It was nice just being here, waiting for you, taking care of the dogs, getting supper ready. Nicer now that you're home. Like old times."

I sipped the wine, my gaze lowered.

He said, "Look at me for a minute, Rainey." His voice sounded serious.

Reluctantly, I raised my eyes. "Do we have to do this now, Buck? It's really been a pretty rotten day."

But his gaze was uncompromising. "I want you to tell me something. How come, do you suppose, we never got divorced? The second time, I mean."

I shrugged uncomfortably. "I don't know. It just seemed kind of stupid, I guess. Like a waste of good money."

"Well, I know." His fingers laced through mine and closed. "For me at least. It's because I'm crazy about you. I always have been. I always will be. But here's the thing, Raine. I need to know where this is going. Where *we're* going. Because I don't think I can keep on like this any longer."

I stared at him, puzzled. "Why?" I said. "Why do we have to go anywhere? Why can't things be the way they are?"

His fingers left mine and reached into his shirt pocket. He said, "I've been keeping something of yours. I need to know whether or not you want it back."

When his palm opened, he was holding a wedding band . . . his grandmother's wedding band, the one I had returned to him on the day I told him that our marriage was over. For the second time.

I looked at the ring in his open hand. But I made no move to take it.

I said huskily, "You know I love you, Buck." I tried to

smile, gesturing with my wineglass. "Look at you. Look at this. What's not to love? But . . ."

"But," he repeated flatly. He lowered his hand.

At length I raised pleading eyes to him. "It's been good these past few months. Why can't we just keep things like they are?"

Slowly he shook his head. "Because I'm closer to forty than thirty. I've waited for you since I was sixteen years old. Sometimes I think waiting for you has gotten to be such a habit that I don't know how to do anything else anymore.

"I know I made mistakes. I know losing you was my fault. My head was messed up back then, but it's not anymore. I want to be married, Raine. I want someone to take care of, someone who cares about me, and I want to do it right this time. I want that someone to be you. But if it can't be . . . I need to get on with my life. I'm tired of being alone. I can't do this anymore, Rainey. And that's the truth."

I said, through lips that were suddenly dry, "I can't go through it again, Buck. I just can't. I guess I'm gun-shy. But I don't trust you. I don't think I ever will." I swallowed hard, dreading to look at him, making myself. "That's the truth."

His hand closed over the ring. "So," he said.

"So," I said.

"I guess that's it."

I placed my hand, quickly and lightly, atop his. "It doesn't mean things have to change between us, Buck. I mean, the way they are now . . . it's nice. Nicer than when we lived together, even. Maybe this is the way it

should be. Maybe this is the only way we're good together."

"Maybe," he agreed. A regretful smile crossed his
lips. "But it's not enough for me."

I didn't understand what that meant. I didn't *want* to
understand.

He stood. I scrambled to my feet after him. "You're
not leaving, are you? Aren't you going to stay and eat?"

"Nah." His voice was casual, but the slight movement
he made to tuck the wedding ring back into his pocket
broke my heart. "I think I'll go on home. You enjoy it,
though. Bring the dishes back sometime."

"Buck." I hurried after him to the door, and I couldn't
believe how selfish the next words sounded. "Are you
still going to help set up for the Pet Fair Saturday?"

He smiled and brushed my hair with a kiss. "Six a.m.,
okay?"

He held out his hand, and it took me a minute to realize he was waiting for his keys. I handed them over.

A blast of cold air entered the room when he opened
the door, and it lingered long after he was gone. I snug-
gled up on the sofa with Cisco and even put another log
on the fire. But I couldn't seem to get warm.

Chapter Eleven

There is nothing more exhilarating than a mountain fair on a crisp cobalt day. The entire downtown area had been cordoned off and was filled with colorful booths. The air smelled of boiled peanuts and hickory-smoked barbecue, and a bluegrass band played on a truck-bed stage. There were caramel apples, caramel corn, corn on the cob and fried pies. A booth sold homemade pies, cakes and breads, and another sold sparkling mason jars filled with red pepper jelly, bread and butter pickles and strawberry jam. There were handcrafted birdhouses, laurel tables, painted signs and exquisite jewel-toned quilts. But most of all there were tourists, oohing and aahing over our quaint mountain crafts and peeling out folding cash to take home souvenirs. The Hansonville Fall Festival was the biggest event of the year.

The Pet Fair had taken over the entire town square, thanks to the charm and determination of Dolly Amstead. This highly desirable piece of real estate—almost a half acre of grass shaded by a giant oak tree whose reddish orange display made it the most attractive feature at the fair—was now decorated with yellow and blue agility equipment, white PVC jumps and festive white lattice ring gating.

A bright blue canopy shaded animal pens where adoptable kittens and puppies romped amidst cedar shavings, and another housed the ticket and donation booth, where for two dollars you could take your pet through a modified agility course—under my supervision, of course—enter a variety of pet contests or sign your dog up for any number of games. For absolutely free you could receive a stack of literature on our proposed new animal shelter and make a donation to the cause. Dolly manned the loudspeaker, announcing upcoming events and rallying enthusiasm for the homeless pets. In between announcements she zipped back and forth among adoptions, ticket sales and events, straightening flyers and tweaking displays and making certain that there was absolutely no doubt in anyone's mind as to who was in charge.

"That woman," muttered Maude, "is giving me a headache."

"Well, you've got to hand it to her," I replied absently. "She does know how to organize."

Maude gave me an odd look. I knew it wasn't like me to miss an opportunity to complain about Dolly, but I really wasn't in the mood. My eyes kept scanning the crowd for Buck. It wasn't that I had anything to say to him, in particular. I don't know why I kept looking for him.

He had helped me load and set up the equipment just

like he promised, and he was his usual easygoing self. But things were awkward and strained between us, and he seemed distant. Or perhaps it was just me.

"Ladies and gentlemen, ladies and gentlemen," Dolly squawked from the loudspeaker. "Three minutes until the agility demonstration! Gather round the square, everyone, for the agility demonstration!"

Maude said, "Looks like you're on."

Cisco was lying under the table with his leash clipped to my chair, panting happily and observing everything that was happening. Hero, on the other hand, lay in a covered crate with his head on his paws, giving absolutely no indication that he had the slightest bit of interest in his surroundings. I would have loved to have given a demonstration of his extraordinary skills for the crowd, but I didn't want to risk stressing him.

So I unsnapped Cisco's leash and led him inside the gated agility ring. Since I had designed the course, it was easy to make him look good. I took him through only the obstacles that he did well and at lightning speed, and we finished with one of his favorite tricks—a victory leap through a circle that I made of my arms. The crowd loved that, and we took a bow.

"Raine Stockton and Cisco, everyone! Wasn't that great? Buy your tickets at the table under the blue tent and Raine will show you and your dog how to do the same thing! Don't forget, all the proceeds from your tickets go to help Hanover County's homeless animals, so line up!"

Dolly's megaphoned voice faded into the background as I made my way back to the table, laughing and waving to my friends, Cisco bouncing along beside me. Maude was already tearing off tickets and taking money, so I quickly ducked down to secure Cisco's leash so that I could help her.

A not-quite-familiar voice said over my head, "It's not exactly the Kentucky Derby, but if you're taking bets I'll put two dollars on the yellow dog's nose."

I straightened up slowly. "Well, as I live and breathe. If it isn't Mr. Miles Young. Slumming?"

He smiled at me. "Just trying to get to know my neighbors."

He was wearing khaki trousers, a navy blazer and an Atlanta Braves baseball cap. He might have passed for an ordinary tourist, if you didn't look too closely. He would never be mistaken for a local.

"I'd like to thank you, Mr. Young, for the five thirty wake-up call your heavy-equipment trucks have been kind enough to give me every day this week. Not to mention the lovely sound of bulldozers scraping off the top of the mountain."

He said, "I thought country people got up early in the morning."

"I own a dog kennel, Mr. Young. When one dog wakes up, everyone wakes up. I like to postpone that until at least sunrise whenever I can."

He looked thoughtful. "Well. I guess I'll just have to build a new road to access my property, then, so I won't have to disturb you and your dogs with all those loud trucks and bulldozers and such."

I stared at him, thinking for a moment he might be serious. But then I saw the quirk of his lips and I said briskly, "Do you have a dog, Mr. Young?"

"No."

"Then you probably don't want to buy a ticket to run this agility course. So if you'll excuse me . . ."

"I had a Chihuahua once," he said, following me over to the ticket table. "At least my ex-wife did. It was a nasty little thing. Bit everything that moved."

Maude handed me a fistful of tickets, barely glancing at Miles Young. "We have instructions from the top to clear the field five minutes before the next demo and we've synchronized watches at"—she glanced at the big sports watch on her wrist—"nine forty-three mark fourteen. So you'd best get started."

Miles Young said, "Good morning, ma'am, I'm Miles Young."

"How do you do," replied Maude. "Would you like to buy a ticket? Each ticket is worth one run through or two minutes on the field."

I shouted, "Number one!"

The first three ticket holders were students of mine, which made matters easy because I did not have to guide their dogs across the dog walk or teach them how to persuade a dog to jump over a bar when he would really rather go around it. The disadvantage of that was that I had no reason to go on the field, and every time I turned around Miles Young was at my shoulder.

"Do you want something?" I demanded.

"Just the pleasure of watching a professional at work."

"You're in my way."

He took an elaborate step back. He had an annoyingly pleasant face—regular features, easy eyes, smarmy smile. It probably served him well to lure his victims into his confidence in high-stakes business deals, but I was not that easily impressed. He said, "Reese Pickens told me you were one to keep an eye on."

"You want to be careful about listening to anything Reese Pickens says." I shouted, "Next!"

A little girl with a basset hound came up and presented her ticket. I was more than happy to leave my post at the entry gate and patiently guide the lumbering flop-eared dog over one jump and up and over a low ramp. When I returned, Miles Young was still there.

"What do you want from me?" I demanded.

His eyes crinkled with that Bahamas tan as he smiled at me. "What makes you think I want anything? Maybe I just think you're cute."

I eyed him suspiciously. "Are you drunk?"

"Actually, I don't drink. My father was an alcoholic," he added, as though I cared. "He was always landing in jail and then calling my uncle, who was the mayor, to come bail him out. Not a particularly nice way to grow up, but I did learn a couple of valuable things from him. The first is: Don't drink. The second is: It pays to have friends in powerful places."

That smarmy smiled never wavered; those crinkly eyes never faded. I felt every muscle in my body stiffen and I replied coldly, "Is that supposed to be some kind of threat? Because I don't particularly consider you powerful, and I will *never* be your friend."

An eyebrow arched slightly beneath the brim of his

baseball cap. "Actually, you're the person in powerful places I was talking about."

My confusion displayed itself in a scowl, and he explained, "Your name comes up a lot. Seems like you're related to, or friends with, just about everyone around here. People listen to what you have to say. It makes me think you would be a good person to have on my side. And," he added, "I do happen to think you're cute."

"You," I told him with great deliberation, "are delusional."

"Is this man bothering you, Raine?"

"Speaking of people in powerful places," Miles Young said, and turned with a grin. "How are you, Sonny?"

I was glad to see that, though she used a metal walking stick and had combed her bangs forward to hide the bruise on her forehead, Sonny displayed no other ill effects from her fall. Of course, I also knew that her long sleeves, colorful knit poncho and ankle-length suede skirt hid a multitude of bruises. "Hello, Miles," she returned pleasantly. "Enjoying a day in the country, are you?"

He nodded appreciatively. "I think I'm really going to like it here."

"Well, don't get too comfortable. Your plan still hasn't passed the water commission."

"No," he agreed, still smiling, "but it's passed everything else."

"Are you in line?" she inquired, tipping her head toward me.

"Afraid not."

"Good, because Mystery wants to run the agility

course." She handed me a ticket. "See you in court, Miles."

"Have a good day, Sonny." He turned to me and added, "You too, Miss Stockton."

"You were awfully nice to that creep," I muttered as he left.

Sonny chuckled. "Oh, he's not so bad. I've known a lot worse, believe me." She handed me Mystery's leash. "Now let's give Mystery her money's worth. The dancing dog is going on pretty soon and I don't want to miss it."

I have to admit, I was skeptical about the dancing dog. It sounded too much like a circus act to me, which is not to take anything away from the skill that's required to train a dog for the circus or any other entertainment venue. It's just that the whole thing seemed a little cutesy-pie, and put me in mind of poodles in tutus hopping around on their hind legs.

After all, dogs are creatures of great nobility and dignity. They plunge into turbulent seas to rescue fishermen; they cross the frozen tundra with life-saving serum; they dig through the rubble of collapsed buildings and snowy avalanches to find helpless victims. It was the domesticated dog who, by assisting early man in the hunt, by protecting his villages and guarding his flocks, made it possible for humans to have enough leisure time to build the Golden Gate Bridge and paint the Sistine Chapel. It could be said that we owe civilization as we know it entirely to the domestic dog.

I am therefore fundamentally against anything that demeans or diminishes the dignity of the dog in any way.

And that, I'm sorry to say, was what I had always imagined canine musical freestyle did.

I couldn't have been more wrong.

Thanks to Dolly's megaphoned promotion, practically everyone at the fair had gathered around the roped-off town square to watch the performance. Had Maude and I not already secured our front-row seats underneath the blue canopy by virtue of our jobs, we would have been standing out in the sun with everyone else, fighting for a spot near the ropes. Sonny sat beside us, holding Mystery in her lap.

Dolly blared from the megaphone, "And now, ladies and gentlemen, Sandra Lanier and the incredible Ringo!"

Out onto the field strode a young woman in tight black satin pants and a long, floaty gold-and-white top. Her blond hair was caught back from her face in a wreath of gold and white flowers, then tumbled over her shoulders. Beside her trotted a dog that might have been a collie–golden retriever mix. The gold and white of his coat was an almost exact match for the gold and white of her top. His head was turned attentively up to his mistress, his eyes never leaving hers, his pawfalls in perfect synchronization with her steps. Maude and I exchanged a look, partly in secret comment on the outfit, partly in genuine admiration for the obedience skills of the dog.

From the sound system came a harp chord, and the woman made a sweeping curtsy to her dog. On the second harp chord the dog returned a gorgeous, perfectly cued bow to her. A chorus of *Ah*s went up from the audience. The recorded orchestra broke into a spritely rendition of

Vivaldi's "Spring" and the two of them took off, moving as a single poetic unit in a ballet of perfectly synchronized turns, spins, leaps and twirls. She floated across the grass, her filmy gold-and-white top fluttering and billowing in a reflection of her dog's flowing coat. They moved first in counterpoint, then in unison. When she turned, he turned with her; when she spun, he spun opposite, forming a beautiful figure eight that met in the middle. He seemed to know, without a visible cue, when she was going to kick into a jeté, and he would dash between her legs while she was practically in midair, or leap over her backward-extended leg, circle her body and pick up on her heel side with his paws striking the ground in precise harmony with the beat of the music. It was incredible. At first I actually had to press my hand against my lips to stifle gasps and cheers like the ones that were coming from every tourist in the crowd, but before the performance was over I was clapping and cheering and crying out with delight just like everyone else. Cisco, puzzled by my behavior but clearly intrigued, put his front paws on the ring gating and barked out his own cheers to the canine half of the dance team.

"Oh, my God, oh, my *God*," I exclaimed as Sandra Lanier was taking her second bow. "I've never seen anything like that in my life, have you?"

Maude nodded crisply. "Well-done," she said. This, for her, was the equivalent of a standing ovation. "Quite."

Sonny was wiping moisture from her cheeks, and she wasn't the only one. "Beautiful," she said, laughing even as she dabbed tears. "Whoever would have thought dogs

could do something like that? It makes you wonder what
else is possible, doesn't it?"

I think that summed up my own feelings exactly.

I pushed myself forward as Sandra Lanier and Ringo
left the ring. "Hi," I said, holding out my hand. "You
were incredible, unbelievable. Thank you so much.
Thank you so much for doing this."

She laughed as she shook my hand, and I realized I
must sound like a gushing twelve-year-old at a rock con-
cert. "Thanks," she said. "We really love it."

"I'm Raine Stockton."

"Sandy Lanier," she said.

"I own a dog-training business just outside of town,"
I went on. "This is Cisco. He does search and rescue." I
hoped I didn't sound as though I was trying too hard to
give myself some legitimacy.

"How do you do, Cisco?"

I liked the fact that she greeted my dog, and that she
added, "Do you mind if Ringo says hello?"

"I think Cisco would be honored."

The two dogs did their sniffing ritual, and she said, "I
saw you earlier in the agility demo. I'll bet Cisco would
be great in freestyle."

"He probably would be, but he has a handicap—me.
Are you a professional dancer?"

She laughed. "Good heavens, no. I'm a physical therapist. I learned to dance for Ringo."

"Gorgeous dog," I said.

"Yes," she said, and turned a gaze on him that was so
full of adoration that I knew immediately how they had
achieved such harmony on the dance floor. "He is. I got

him from the shelter when he was three months old. I could tell from the first he was going to be special."

Cisco, with his usual happy-go-lucky manners, gave a grinning, invitational bark and play-bowed to Ringo. Sandy laughed. "See, he already has a move!" She looked at me, eyes twinkling. "Would you like me to show you some more?"

I was sucked in. The mere thought of being able to do something as beautiful as I had just seen was an irresistible temptation. Before I knew it the crowd had moved back to form a small circle and we were at the center of it. Armed with a training clicker and a plastic baggie filled with chopped hot dogs—already I liked her style, and so did Cisco—Sandy Lanier proceeded to teach my handsome working dog how to dance. In a matter of moments she had him spinning at my side, weaving through my legs, and—his apparent favorite—twirling on his hind legs.

"Great," I commented wryly as Cisco launched himself to his back legs and spun around yet again, eagerly anticipating his hot dog reward. "I've been trying to teach him to turn off a light switch all week, but he refuses to stand on his hind legs. What have you got that I don't?"

She laughed. "Some dogs just dance to a different drummer."

In the distance, the bluegrass band struck up "Turkey in the Straw," and Sandy bowed to me, her eyes filled with mirth. "Shall we dance?"

Before I knew it, Cisco and I were performing a hilarious square dance duet with Sandy and Ringo, weaving, crossing, allemanding and spinning. Most of the time I was laughing so hard I didn't care where my feet were, and the rest of the time I was either bumping into Sandy or tripping over Cisco, but my dog was having the time of his life. The crowd was clapping in rhythm and hooting their encouragement, and a photographer snapped our picture for the paper. When the music stopped, we really hammed it up, bowing and posing and blowing kisses. Then I caught a glimpse of Buck, standing at the edge of the crowd watching us, and the look in his eyes was so sad, so unguarded and lost, that the laughter died in my throat.

Suddenly I didn't feel like dancing anymore.

"Come on," I told Sandy. "I'll buy you a Coke."

We made our way back to the blue tent amidst grinning applause, Cisco bounding happily around me, and Ringo, as attentive as ever, glued to Sandy's side.

"I think Cisco missed his calling," Sonny said as we approached. "He should have been on Broadway."

I introduced her to Sandy, and Sonny said, "You were marvelous. I can't tell you when I've been so moved. Did it take you long to learn?"

They chatted while I fished some soft drinks out of the cooler underneath the table. I handed one to Sandy and another to Sonny.

Sonny was asking, "Are you going to be in the area long?"

"I'm heading out to do some hiking tomorrow," Sandy said. She perched on the edge of the table and popped the top of her soft drink. "Ringo and I like to spend a week on the trail every autumn."

"Oh, yeah?" I sat beside her. "What part do you hike?"

"We generally get on the Lovitt-Hugh Trail at Beacham Falls and follow it until it intersects the Appalachian at Devil's Knob. Then we take the Appalachian Trail back down to High Point station."

"Sounds great." I sighed, fleetingly jealous. A week on the trail in the crisp yellow autumn, with nothing but clear mountain air and breathtaking mountain views everywhere I looked, and no one but my dog for company. But then I remembered that no matter how frantic my life seemed now and then, I had all of this beauty whenever I wanted it, while she only got to visit once a year.

"Are you staying in town tonight?" Sonny asked.

"I haven't decided yet," replied Sandy, swinging her crossed ankles. "I passed a hotel that takes dogs on the way into town, or we may get a campsite."

"I understand Cisco has a new career," said Maude from behind us. She had Hero on a lead beside her. "I'm sorry to have missed the performance, but I thought this fellow needed a little exercise."

She extended her hand to Sandy. "You, my dear, were exquisite. Gorgeous attention on that dog. I'm Maude Braselton, and it is a pleasure."

Sandy beamed as she hopped down from the table. "Thank you. Everyone has been so kind. And I've had a great time with Raine and Cisco."

Suddenly Hero barked. We all looked at him, startled, but were even more surprised to see his tail wagging madly, his eyes alert and his mouth open in a panting smile.

Sandy exclaimed, "Well, hello! And who is this handsome fellow?"

"His name is Hero," I said, "and he certainly seems to like you."

She knelt and began stroking Hero's head and ears. He practically melted at her touch. I hadn't seen him so animated since I'd taken him from the cabin a week ago.

"Actually," I corrected myself, "his real name is Nero. We're just fostering him until someone can come and get him. He's a service dog," I explained, "whose owner was killed. He has to go back to the agency that provided him."

Her hands had stopped stroking Hero, and she looked up at me with a flicker of shock in her eyes. "Killed?" she repeated.

I nodded. "Murdered, in one of the cabins on the lake last week. The poor dog was trapped inside for days before anyone realized what had happened."

"How . . . awful." She sounded as horrified as I felt even now, when I told the story. She stood slowly, staring at Hero. He gazed up at her, tail wagging, eyes bright, and whined.

"You might have heard about it on the radio," I added. "Her name was Mickey White."

She kept staring at Hero. "No," she said. "I don't . . . I didn't hear. I have to go," she said abruptly, and her smile seemed forced and strained. "It was nice meeting you. All of you." A vague glance that met no one's eyes. "Ringo, with me."

Ringo took up perfect heel position beside her and the two of them left without another word.

Sonny, Maude and I looked at each other in confusion, but no one said anything. No one, that is, except Hero, who turned in the direction Sandy had gone, and barked.

"I tell you," Sonny said, stroking Hero's head as it rested on her knee, "she reminded him of something. Happier times."

"Well, I don't know about that," I said, "but he certainly seems happier now. I think he likes you." Of course, all animals liked Sonny. Whether she could actually talk to them or not, she did hold an undeniable charm over almost all living things.

"I like him too," Sonny said, smiling down at the Lab as she massaged his ears. "He's such a serious fellow, though. I wish I could make him laugh."

"Dogs don't laugh."

"Of course they do. Cisco was laughing the whole time he was dancing with you."

"Oh, great. Even my *dog* was laughing at me."

"Dogs laugh when they're having fun, just like we do. This guy needs to have more fun. Even Mystery thinks so."

"Border collies think everyone needs to have more fun."

"That girl, Sandy, reminded him of when he used to have fun," Sonny said thoughtfully, gazing down at Hero. "Times when he was with his mistress. Times when he was working. That's why he was so excited to see her."

The purple shadows were growing long and the vendors were packing up. Maude was loading the car and exercising the dogs before putting them inside. Sonny and I counted the receipts from the Pet Fair while Dolly bustled around giving orders to everyone who didn't have sense enough to look busy. Buck had gotten a friend to help him pack up the agility equipment and take it back to my house. Tangled bunting and overflowing trash cans were the last forlorn remnants of a perfect golden day.

I had asked Buck, as a way of thanking him for his help and in a rather pathetic attempt to reestablish the norm, if he wanted to have dinner. He had replied, as pleasant as ever, that he'd already promised Wyn they'd go for barbecue. They often did that after working a shift, and they often invited me. I waited, but no invitation came.

Wyn would have brought it up if she had been standing there. I got the feeling that Buck was glad she was not. I tried not to be depressed.

"Dogs don't have much of a long-term memory," I reminded Sonny.

"You just saw a dog perform a ballet to Vivaldi," Sonny replied, deadpan. "Do you want to rethink that statement?"

I shrugged. "Well, I admit, he did perk up when he saw her."

"I think he recognized her."

I looked at her, thoughtful. "It's possible," I admitted.

"Dolly said Sandy and Ringo go all over the Carolinas performing. It wouldn't be much of a stretch to think Mickey and Hero might have seen her at some event or another."

"And that would have had happy memories for him."

I said with a sigh, "Too bad they didn't last." As soon as Sandy had disappeared from sight, the Lab had returned to his former despondent mood. He hadn't cheered up until Sonny had called him over to sit with her and Mystery while she helped me with the receipts.

"He's just so lost," Sonny said. "He doesn't know what he's supposed to be now. And he feels responsible. He says if he had been a better dog, his woman would still be with him, and he'd still be helping her."

I wished she wouldn't say things like that. Sometimes they made too much sense not to be true.

She looked at me and seemed to hesitate. "There's something else," she said. "I wasn't going to mention it, because it doesn't really add up. An animal that traumatized, that confused . . . you can't expect him to understand anything that's happened. But today I got the oddest impression from him. I ignored it at first, but he seemed certain, almost urgent." Her tone was apologetic, but her eyes held mine with the conviction of what she relayed. "He seems to think," she said, "he *insists* that it was a snake that killed his mistress."

I said, "It was a gun that killed his mistress."

"Or a snake with a gun."

"I don't think dogs are metaphorical."

"You don't think dogs can talk to people," she pointed

out, "or that I can talk to them." Then she shrugged. "Of course, maybe I'm misunderstanding."

"Maybe," I agreed, and in a way I was glad to hear something this nonsensical coming from one of her purported communications with the animals. It was a lot easier to believe she did *not* know what she was talking about at times like these.

"It's just that I keep getting the same picture," she said, "and I know it's coming from him." She unfolded a piece of paper that was stuck in among the dollar bills in the donation jar and glanced at it. "It's the same . . . Oh, my goodness."

I looked up from my work with the calculator. She was staring at the paper. "What?"

She said in the same kind of stunned voice, "Dolly is going to wet her pants."

"What? What is it?"

"This." With an effort, she tore her eyes away from the paper and met mine. "It's a check. From Miles Young."

She turned it around to face me. The amount scrawled across the front in bold flowing letters was *Fifty Thousand Dollars*.

I reached my hand out for it, as though to verify the authenticity.

"Read the note in the memo," Sonny said.

I did, and my face grew hot. It said: *Raine and Cisco— thanks for the dance.*

Chapter Twelve

The weather turned cold and rainy on Sunday, and the drizzle lasted through Monday. The tourists went home. The bulldozers didn't come. The leaves blew off the trees and we all were reminded that, as festive as autumn was, winter inevitably followed.

I tried to give equal training time to Cisco and to Hero. Cisco, a retriever after all, should have taken to the "take and return" command far more quickly than he did, and I admit it was frustrating to work with him. He had no problem retrieving a stuffed toy, a ball or a knotted rope, but when it came to the telephone receiver, my purse or a pill bottle, he just didn't see the point. On the other hand, he couldn't wait to show me his new freestyle tricks and interpreted every "down" command as a chance to show off his rollover, and every "up" cue as an opportunity to twirl on his hind legs. In my glummest moments I actually wondered whether his brief exposure to dancing might have ruined him as a working dog.

And I admit, I was glum. I hated not hearing from Buck. I hated not being able to just pick up the phone and talk to him, or stop by his house for a beer, or meet him in town for a bite. I hated his not being there, at the periphery of my life or in the center of it, cheering me on or steering me straight. It was like having your best friend mad at you.

"I'm just so tired of breaking up with him," I told Maude dispiritedly. Most of our boarders had gone home, and we were taking the opportunity to scrub down the kennels with suds and hot water, floor to ceiling. This was never my favorite job, but today I was glad to have something physical to do; something from which I could see immediate results for my labor. "It seems like I've spent most of my life either falling in love with him or breaking up with him."

Maude, wise woman that she was, said nothing, but vigorously applied a long-handled scrub brush to a wall.

"I just don't understand why it has to be all or nothing with him all of a sudden," I went on, wringing out a mop in the kennel across the aisle from her. "God knows that never seemed to be his motto when we were married." I applied the mop to the floor with particular vengeance. It made a satisfying slapping sound.

"He says he's getting older," I continued. "Like I'm not? But that doesn't mean I'm getting stupider as well. I mean, how many times do you have to make the same mistake before you finally say—*Duh!* Maybe I shouldn't do that anymore? Isn't that the definition of crazy? To keep doing the same thing over and over again and expect different results? Do you know what I think his problem is? I think—"

The sharp trilling of the telephone interrupted my tirade. Maude said, "Hold that thought, my dear. Really, I'm on tenterhooks." She pressed the button on the cordless extension we brought into the kennel area from the office. "Dog Daze. May I help you?"

I made a face at her and turned back to my scrubbing. But in another moment she had handed the phone to me. I wiped my soapy hands on my jeans before accepting it.

"Raine Stockton."

"Miss Stockton, this is David Kines. I'm Mickey White's father. And also"—he seemed to rush on before I could interject with my sympathies—"the executor of her estate. I understand you've been keeping my daughter's dog."

I said, "Yes, sir. I'm so sorry for your loss. I have your card, and I was going to call you. I've been in touch with the service dog agency, and they tell me their contract with your daughter requires that the dog be turned over to them for placement."

He said brusquely, "Yes, that's what they tell me too."

"Of course, if you wanted to adopt him as a pet, I'm sure—"

"Got no use for dogs," he interrupted. "Don't mean to interfere. Just trying to settle things up. If you've got a bill for keeping him, I want to let you know where to send it."

I said, "There's no charge, Mr. Kines. I'm happy to help."

"Don't need charity, either. My Mickey always paid her own way. I mean to abide by her wishes."

This threw me off balance a little. "It's not charity, Mr. Kines. It's just what I do."

Maude threw me a questioning look, and I shrugged an answer.

"I'm sending you a check for five hundred dollars," he said shortly. "That ought to cover it."

"Please, there's no need—"

"Young lady, do you know who I am?"

I said, "Pardon me?"

He said, "I am David Andrew Kines, president and CEO of the largest textile manufacturer in the state of Tennessee. I take care of my own, do you understand that? I take care of my own."

And with that, the connection clicked off.

I stared at Maude. "Ho-ly cow," I said, returning the phone. "He's sending me five hundred dollars."

"Who is?"

"Mickey White's father."

"He sounds like a gentleman."

I answered uneasily, "Not really."

And later that afternoon, my suspicions were borne out.

The second phone call came as I was locking up the sparkling clean and disinfected-to-within-an-inch-of-its-life kennel. I walked Maude to her car, hunched inside my canvas barn coat, stepping around cold brown puddles that gave off feeble reflections of the day's dying light.

"Are you sure you don't want to come over later for a bite to eat?" Maude said.

"Thanks," I said, trying not to sound despondent. "Buck left some stew the other night. I put it in the freezer. Maybe I'll warm it up."

She opened her car door and turned to me. "I've known you and Buck as long as you've known each other," she said, "and it seems to me that you both enjoy the chase more than the capture. Not just Buck," she said pointedly, "both of you. Maybe you've grown out of that, maybe you haven't. But you've got an awful lot of years invested in each other. It might be prudent to invest another hour or two talking to each other before tossing it all away, don't you think?"

I hugged her, and she got into her car.

I was walking back to the kennel building to lock up when I heard the phone ringing inside. I hurried to answer it.

It was Letty Cranston again.

"Oh, Mrs. Cranston, you just missed her!" I hurried to the door to make sure, but there was no sign of Maude's dusty Volvo. "Do you have her home phone?" I gave her the number and added, "I'm so glad you called back, though. We were disconnected last time before you gave me a number, and the sheriff's department has been trying to reach you."

"My dear, don't I know it!" she exclaimed. "I must have a dozen messages! What is going on? I certainly can't be wanted for any crime up that way. I haven't even been there in twenty years!"

I knew it probably wasn't my place to relay the news,

but I honestly couldn't be sure the authorities would ever be able to talk to her in Crete. I said, "I'm sorry to have to tell you this, but the woman who was renting your cabin, Mickey White, was shot to death there last week. Her husband was found a few days later at the bottom of a ravine. He hit his head and drowned in the creek."

Her silence was brief, and when she spoke her tone was brisk and matter-of-fact. "Well, I can't say I'm surprised. That husband of hers was a no-account loafer who was born to meet a bad end, and Mickey—well, God bless her for her disability and all, but she couldn't have been the easiest person in the world to live with."

"How well did you know them, Mrs. Cranston?"

"Oh, they've been renting the cabin from me for about three years now, every October. My next-door neighbor in Florida is Mickey's aunt; that's how I got to know them. Poor Amelia, she must be just heartbroken. I'll have to call her. She talked about Mickey all the time. Not having any children of her own, don't you know, she more or less adopted Mickey. She came to visit once or twice—Mickey did—and what a pill. Always demanding this and insisting on that. And that husband of hers, 'Yes, dear'-ing her all over the place. I tell you the truth, it plumb got on my nerves after a while. Hard to believe he did what he did. But the dog was nice," she added, in a slightly cheerier tone. "Smartest dog I've ever seen."

I homed in on what she'd said earlier. "What do you mean? What did her husband do?"

"Oh." She seemed taken aback, as though she too were trying to rethink the conversation. "He had an affair, don't you know. Who would think he had the gumption?"

"No kidding," I said, trying to encourage her to keep gossiping. "When?"

"Oh, Lord, it had Amelia in such a tizzy this summer. The worst of it was that Mickey's father found out and actually threatened to have Leo killed! Well, not threatened so much as promised. And if anyone could do it, that man could. He's got money, and some friends in low places, if you know what I mean. Why, I hear tell"—a burst of static interrupted her, and I rejoined the conversation as she was saying—"therapist, if you can believe that. As far as I know, that put an end to Leo's roving eye. But like I said, it doesn't surprise me a bit, the way things ended up."

"Therapist?" I repeated. "You mean, like a marriage counselor? What—" More static, loud enough for me to be forced to remove the telephone receiver from my ear.

I said quickly, "Mrs. Cranston, I think we're about to lose the connection. Could you give me your cell phone number? I know the police will want to talk to you. Are you still out of the country?"

She acknowledged that she was, and read off a series of numbers, which I copied down faithfully.

She said, "But the person I really need to talk to is Marsha Lee, who is supposed to be managing that place for me. Somebody's got to get in there and—"

More static.

I said, "I don't think the police are letting anyone in. It's a crime scene, you know. But I can have them call you as soon as they release it. Mrs. Cranston? Mrs. Cranston?"

I was talking to dead air.

I pushed the OFF button on the phone, waited for a dial tone and excitedly dialed the sheriff's department. This was the kind of thing I would usually eagerly share with Buck, but when the dispatcher answered I found myself instead asking for my uncle Roe. With sudden insight, I knew that if I was going to be the one to break the ice between Buck and myself, it should be with a topic that did not involve police work.

"Sorry, Raine, he went home early," replied the dispatcher. "You want me to patch you through?"

"Yes, thanks. Wait," I added. "Take down this number for whoever is working the Mickey White case." I knew that at least one of those people was Buck. "The state police might want it too. It's for Letty Cranston, in Crete. Yeah, that's near Greece."

I gave her the number, and she said, "Crete, wow. Love to be there on a day like today, wouldn't you?" I agreed it would be nice, and she rang through to my uncle's house.

I counted eight rings and was just about to hang up when my aunt answered. I was so excited that at first I didn't even notice her distracted tone or the voices in the background.

"Hi, Aunt Mart," I said. "Listen, is Uncle Roe around? I've got some important—"

"Raine! Raine!" Her voice was high and thin and on the verge of hysteria, and then I knew something was wrong. "Thank God you called. I've got to go. They're taking him now. I've got to go."

"What?" I demanded, and I felt coldness creep through my fingertips. "Taking who? What's wrong?"

"Roe," she said, sobbing. "They're taking him in the ambulance. They think it's his heart."

I spent the next six hours in the ICU waiting room of Middle Mercy Hospital, holding my aunt's hand, bringing her coffee, making telephone calls. I called the pastor, my cousin Kate in Chicago, who was Aunt Mart and Uncle Roe's oldest child, and Maude. The pastor was at the hospital within half an hour, and Maude wanted to come, but I asked her instead to simply take care of the dogs in case I didn't make it home by morning. Aunt Mart refused to let Kate make a flight reservation until she knew more about my uncle's condition.

I kept trying to call Buck, both because, as ranking member of the sheriff's department he needed to know the situation, and because I needed him. He needed to be here, with me, and with Aunt Mart. His home phone kept ringing through to voice mail, and his cell phone was apparently turned off. I knew it was his day off, but I was furious with him for not letting me know where he was going, for not being there when I needed him. I *always* knew where he was, just like he always knew where I was. It wasn't right, this estrangement. How dare he do this to me; how dare he desert me when I needed him most? I was so upset, so frustrated and helpless, that I could almost even blame him for Uncle Roe's heart attack.

Finally I gave up and called the office, leaving it up to the dispatcher to spread the word to the department. Over the next two hours, five deputies showed up to sit with Aunt Mart, but none of them was Buck.

Around midnight, the doctor came in to tell us that it had indeed been a heart attack, but that the damage did not appear to be severe and my uncle was expected to make a full recovery. Aunt Mart and I hugged each other, and the pastor hugged both of us and said a little prayer of thanks. So did I.

"We'll keep him here for a few days," the doctor went on, "but it will be quite a while longer before he can go back to work. Think of this as a warning. We'll be talking about some major lifestyle changes before we send him home."

Aunt Mart demanded, "Can I see him?"

"Just for a minute. He needs his rest."

She returned from my uncle's room beaming and dabbing her eyes with a tissue. "He's as feisty as ever. Not a thing in the world wrong with that man. Already trying to give me a list of things he wants brought to him from the office, like that's going to happen."

One by one the visitors hugged her, promised their availability day or night and departed. For a moment I was confused by how familiar the scene looked: somber-faced friends and men in uniform lined up to embrace and offer comfort, and then I remembered where I had witnessed the same kind of scene before—at the funeral home when first my mother, and then my father died. I was seized by an intense gratitude that this time, the outcome was different.

It was close to three a.m. by the time I got Aunt Mart settled at home and in bed with a sleeping pill the doctor had given her to make sure her rest was uninterrupted. Wearily, I made my way toward my own home and bed.

But there was one stop I had to make first. On impulse, I swung my car onto the narrow dirt road that preceded my own driveway by a couple of miles—the road that led to Buck's house.

To my great relief, I could see both his car and his pickup in the open garage when I swung into the short drive that bisected his yard. He was home. I wasn't in the least bit concerned about waking him before dawn; he would have wanted me to, and besides, he deserved it. Why hadn't he answered his phone?

I left the car door open for light and bounded up his front steps. "Buck!" I pounded on the door. "Buck, wake up, it's me!"

I didn't give him time to get to the door, or even to turn on a light. I tried the door, and it was open, as I knew it would be.

"Buck!" I called again, and hit the light switch by the door. At the same time, I saw a light come on in the bedroom down the hall. I rushed toward it.

"Buck, it's Raine! I've been trying to call you. I—"

I broke off as I rounded the corner and came face to face with Buck at the bedroom door. He was tousle-haired and shirtless, wearing a pair of hastily donned jeans that weren't quite buttoned, and his hand was braced against the door—not to open it, but to close it against me. He need not have bothered.

From my position as I burst into the hallway I had a

perfect view of the rumpled bed and of the woman who struggled to cover herself there. Her face was stricken, and her eyes, as they met mine, conveyed an anguish of humiliation and regret.

I looked at her for a long time. Then I looked at Buck. He closed his eyes slowly against what he must have seen in mine, or perhaps in an effort to mask the emotions that he did not want me to see in his.

I said quietly, "You need to call the office."

And I left.

Chapter Thirteen

"They had him up walking this morning," I told perhaps the sixteenth caller that day. "He's already giving orders and making the nurses crazy. He's going to be just fine." And in response to the inevitable question, I added, "He'll be out of work at least six weeks. After that, I don't know. Thank you. I'll tell him you called."

I hung up the phone and rolled my neck to loosen the stiffness. Sonny, who had actually gotten Hero to play a rather sedate game of fetch with a knotted rope toy, asked, "Who's in charge of the sheriff's department while your uncle's laid up?"

I answered, trying to keep all inflection out of my voice, "Buck."

"Oh," she said, and held my gaze for a moment. "That's . . . complex."

She knew about my early morning encounter with Buck, and so did Maude. The one thing I had never done was evade the truth about Buck's character, not even to protect my own ego. I shrugged. "He's the senior man. I don't know if it's official yet, but somebody has to take over. It'll be him."

I sat down across from Sonny at the kitchen table with a cup of coffee. It was almost noon, and I had lost track of how many cups I'd poured.

Cisco sat beside me and pressed his shoulder insistently into my knee. He hadn't let me out of his sight since I had returned before dawn that morning, and now he couldn't seem to get close enough to me. Dogs hate to have their routines interrupted, and the events of the past twenty-four hours had upset everyone.

Sonny sat back in her chair, her coffee mug cradled in both hands. "Well, I'm just going to say it. I like Buck."

"Everyone does. He's a nice guy."

"I thought you two were good together."

I shrugged. "We were. Most of the time."

"And I just can't believe he did this to you. He should be shot."

"He has a record," I pointed out. "And I don't think shooting him would help."

She covered my hand briefly with hers. "I'm sorry you were hurt. Can I do anything?"

I allowed myself, for one brief moment, to feel a stab of grief. "Know any good lawyers?" I inquired.

Then I glanced down at the coffee, thought about warming it up and decided to drink it as it was. "I'm not hurt," I told her, a little bit surprised to find that it was true. "With everything else that's happened, it actually doesn't seem very important at all. Maybe I feel a little stupid, but I'm not hurt."

What I couldn't entirely put into words was the fact

that what I really felt was relief. It was as though I had been waiting all this time for the other shoe to drop, and now it had. I wasn't surprised, or even disappointed. Of course I had known deep down that the fantasy of saving a marriage that had already been shattered into irreconcilable pieces was just that—a fantasy. I was simply glad that what had once seemed like an impossibly difficult decision had been made for me.

Buck and I had met each other in the corridor of the hospital when I returned a few hours ago; he was entering as I was leaving. We said hello, but that was all.

I shrugged again and added, "I really can't even get mad at him. After all, I knew he was a snake when I picked him up."

She looked puzzled, and I explained, "You know that story about the woman who finds a snake frozen on the ground, then takes him home and thaws him out, and as soon as the snake can move again, he bites her. When she says, 'How could you do that?' the snake says, 'Why are you so surprised? You knew I was a snake when you picked me up.'"

She smiled, and Hero, sitting suddenly at her side, barked. Her smile changed to a kind of puzzled interest as she looked at the dog. I was as startled as she was.

"He hasn't barked once since I brought him here," I said. "And now he suddenly seems to have a lot to say. First he barked at Sandy Lanier, and now at you."

She said, still looking at him, "It was the snake. Something about a snake. He says be careful of the snake."

I sipped the lukewarm coffee. "Thanks, Hero. Too little, too late."

Sonny looked up at me. "He says the snake came, and she died."

I frowned uneasily, and because I never knew how to respond to comments like that, I changed the subject by retrieving the knotted rope from the floor and tossing it gently across the floor. Hero trotted politely after it, and Cisco, watching him, growled lowly. I said sharply to Cisco, "Stop!"

Sonny chuckled. "Cisco says he wishes Hero would just go home."

"I don't need an animal communicator to figure that out," I said. "The guy from the service dog agency is supposed to be here Friday afternoon. But I'm going to miss Hero. And it's such a shame to think of retiring a great dog like that."

"All he wants to do is work," Sonny agreed.

Hero dropped the rope toy into Sonny's lap and looked at her adoringly. She scratched his chin. "I'm going to miss him too. Maybe," she suggested, "I could bring him home with me for a few hours before he goes and let him run with Mystery. She says she likes him almost as much as Cisco."

Cisco growled again, very softly, and Sonny did not help by laughing. "Don't worry, Cisco, no one is trying to take your place. Why is he so insecure?" she asked me.

I made an unpleasant face that was meant to be funny but which came across, I suspect, as rather sad. "He comes from a broken home."

The telephone rang again and I stretched to answer it.

"Raine, hey." It was Rick, my boss at the forest service. "How's your uncle?"

"He's coming home next week. They think he's going to be fine."

"Great news. Modern medicine is really something. Used to be people didn't survive something like that. Do you think he'll stay on as sheriff?"

"I don't know," I admitted. This was a subject on which, for obvious political reasons, I wasn't free to speculate. "The doctor says he'll be out of work for six weeks, though."

"Shame." Rick allowed a respectful silence. Then, as usual, life went on. "Listen, the reason I'm calling is one of the guys found a stray dog out in the woods, looks like it got away from some camper. No collar or ID, and it's kind of a mess, but it seems friendly enough. Hate to think it might be some kid's pet. I know you've got enough on your plate right now, but if you could come by and look at it . . ."

What he really meant was, "If you could come by, pick it up, spring for the vet bills and board it until some unsuspecting soul can be conned into giving it a good home . . ." But what could I say? This is what I *do*.

And life goes on.

I sighed. "Okay, Rick. Hold on to it for a little while longer. I'll head on up that way as soon as I check to see if Aunt Mart needs anything."

He said, "Thanks, Raine. You tell your uncle we all send our best up here, okay?"

"I will, Rick, thanks. See you in a bit."

Sonny was gathering up her things as I hung up.

"Stray dog," I explained, "found on forest service land. I'm going to go pick him up."

"Go on ahead," Sonny said. "I just stopped by to see if I could do anything for you. I'll be happy to take the stray if you need me to."

"Thanks, but I've got plenty of room. The kennels are practically empty. That's why Maude could spare the time to go sit with Aunt Mart at the hospital while I took telephone duty. I appreciate it, though."

Sonny swung her shawl around her shoulders and said, "Call me if you need me." She bent down to pet Hero's head. "See you later, big fellow." She hesitated, and then looked up at me.

"He says," she relayed, almost apologetically, "to watch out for snakes."

I took Cisco with me for the ride to the ranger station. The truth is, the minute I opened the door he dashed through it and was waiting for me with his paws on the door handle of the SUV before I left the front porch. Generally I would not have tolerated that kind of behavior. All my dogs know they are supposed to wait at an open door before being released to cross through it, and everyone but Cisco usually does that. Today I was simply too tired to be a good dog trainer. Besides, I wanted the company.

The rain had lifted, leaving the bite of the passing cold front in the air and a blanket of wispy clouds over the blue shoulders of the mountains. Only a few brave orange and red leaves clung to the limbs of the trees I saw on my way up the mountain, and even the colorful carpet on the forest floor was beginning to look dull.

The crate I use for transporting rescue dogs was in the back of the vehicle, and Cisco rode up front with me. Because—with the outstanding exception of Hero—Cisco was usually very good with other dogs, I took him inside the building with me when I reached the ranger station, although I took the precaution of keeping him on leash. I dropped the leash as soon as I realized there was no one inside but Rick, and let Cisco rush over to receive his petting.

"Well, if it isn't Fred Astaire!" exclaimed Rick, rubbing Cisco's back until his tail whipped back and forth so enthusiastically it looked as though he might take off into orbit. "Let's see some moves, dude, let's see some moves!"

I grimaced. It seemed as though a year had passed since the Pet Fair, instead of only a few days. "You heard about that, huh?"

He looked up at me, laughing. "Everybody's heard about it," he told me. "I understand you've got a few moves of your own. Not thinking about leaving us for the stage, are you?"

"Very funny. Where's the dog?"

"Jimbo's got him out back, trying to knock some of the mud off of him. He doesn't look too bad, but he was out in the rainstorm. We didn't have anything to feed him except half a tuna sandwich. Hope it doesn't make him sick."

"Since he's riding in my car, me too."

We talked for a few minutes about Uncle Roe and life

in general, and I heard the back door open. I made a grab for Cisco's leash, but too late. He gave a happy bark of greeting, and then bounded over to sniff and play-bow to the dog who had just accompanied Jimbo into the room. The dog returned a greeting of his own, and the two canines began circling each other and wiggling and dipping like old friends. There was a good reason for that.

I stared. The dog was wet, tangled and bedraggled, but unmistakable. "Oh, my God," I exclaimed. "Ringo!"

"You don't understand," I insisted to Rick. "This dog is like—well, like Lassie, or somebody! His owner would no more just let him wander off than—than a jockey would forget to lock the stable door of a Triple Crown winner! And no way would Ringo leave her, not of his free will, anyway. Something has to have happened."

"I don't know what to tell you, Raine," replied Rick, replacing the telephone receiver. "I've checked with every station up and down the way, and she didn't check in with any of them. No unaccounted-for vehicles in the parking lots. You said she was an experienced hiker. She's got to know enough to check in with the ranger station before she sets out."

Jimbo came in from the back room. "I checked the access points to the Appalachian Trail, and nobody's seen anyone matching her description, no cars in the parking lot. My guess is she changed her mind."

"Then what was her dog doing running loose in the woods?" I insisted. "Where did you find him, again?"

"Sniffing around the picnic tables at the Number Three campsite," Jimbo said. "But that doesn't mean anything. He could have been traveling for days."

I had to agree with him there. A domestic dog, lost and afraid, will always seek out places where people or other dogs have been, and he will travel great distances to do that. But it was at least a place to start.

I said, "She could be hurt on the trail somewhere. We can't just leave her out there."

Rick said, "You know as well as I do we can't organize a search until someone files a missing-or-overdue report."

"Well, I'm filing one!"

He sighed. "Raine, you don't even know this person. There's absolutely no evidence that she even went hiking. Maybe her plans changed. Maybe the rain scared her off. Wouldn't be the first tourist to hightail it back to the city after one night in a wet sleeping bag."

"She would *not* leave her dog!"

The two men exchanged a look. I focused my attention on Ringo, who, with the excitement of meeting a familiar dog now past, was lying by the door, his head tilted toward me expectantly, as though waiting for his ride home.

Rick said, "Tell you what we'll do. Let's call the radio station, put out an announcement. Ringo, did you say his name was? If she's in the area, chances are she'll hear it and know where to find him. Meanwhile, we'll keep an eye out along the trails, just in case you're right. We already know she didn't show up at either Beechum Falls or High Point station. Maybe she did change her route, or had somebody drive her car to a drop-off point for her. All I'm saying is that until we either have evidence that she actually *did* go hiking, or somebody reports her missing, there's not a whole lot more we can do."

I blew out a frustrated breath. I knew he was right. I said, "Okay. But you don't mind if Cisco and I poke around a little, do you?"

Rick's frown was skeptical. "After the rain? With no place to start? What for?"

I said, "Humor me."

He shrugged. "Knock yourself out. But I don't see how you can expect to get much done today. It'll be going on dark in four hours."

I slipped a loop leash over Ringo's neck. "Call the radio station," I said. "I'm going to take this guy home and start backtracking from the campsite."

"Come on, Raine, don't—"

"Not official," I assured him, and opened the door. "It's just a walk in the woods. I'll be back in half an hour."

Rick called after me, "Don't you have enough to worry about?"

The thing was, he was right. But that was *exactly* why I had to follow through on this, why I couldn't believe the obvious explanation—that Sandy Lanier had simply changed her mind about hiking or lost her dog. Before Uncle Roe's heart attack I had had a theory that had seemed wild at the time. Now it didn't seem so wild.

This was the kind of thing I would usually hash out with Buck. I could call for his input, his assistance, his cool head. I cannot describe the hollow stab of loneliness

I felt in the pit of my stomach when I picked up my cell phone and realized I was no longer free to just dial his number.

Letty Cranston had said something about a *therapist*. Sandy Lanier said she was from Charleston, but her actual address might have been anywhere in the greater Charleston area. Hero *had* recognized her. And she had recognized Hero, when I told her his real name and his occupation. She had gone as white as a sheet when I told her Mickey White had been murdered.

And now she was missing.

I simply wasn't willing to wait until I got home to confirm my hunch. So as soon as I got a signal I pulled off the road into a dirt driveway and rummaged through the console until I found the card Uncle Roe had given me. I dialed the cell phone number of Mickey White's father.

He answered gruffly, "Kines."

I said, "Mr. Kines, this is Raine Stockton from Dog Daze. I'm keeping your daughter's service dog, remember?"

"Listen, I told you I would send you a check. These things take time, miss, and you're on the list just like everybody else. But if you think you can just call up here and—"

I interrupted, "That's not why I'm calling, Mr. Kines."

"Well?" he demanded impatiently.

"I was wondering . . . Do you happen to know the name of your daughter's physical therapist?"

Dead silence was my answer.

"Was her name Sandra Lanier?"

The silence was so long this time that I thought he might have hung up on me. And then he said, in a voice made all the more menacing by its softness, "What in the *hell* business is that of yours?"

I swallowed hard. In for a penny, in for a pound. "Was that who your son-in-law was having an affair with?"

"Who the hell are you, lady?" There was nothing soft about his tone now. I actually winced. "What do you mean, calling me on my cell phone making accusations like that? My daughter is dead, don't you realize that? And that son-of-a-bitch husband of hers killed her!"

I said, "Sandy Lanier is missing, Mr. Kines. Just like your son-in-law was missing, before he was found dead facedown in a creek." I took a breath, and a stab in the dark. "Do you know anything about buying and selling coins over the Internet?"

Dead silence. And then, "Who *are* you?"

"Nobody," I said. "Just a girl with a dog." And, heart pounding, I hung up.

My uncle would kill me if he knew what I had just done, and my Aunt Mart would kill me for telling him. And the truth was, even I couldn't entirely believe I had done it. The part about Sandy Lanier being the woman with whom Leo White was having an affair was a complete stab in the dark, but could I have been *right*? And was it such a stretch to think that a man like Kines, with money and power and "friends in low places," as Letty Cranston had said, might be involved in some almost-legal Internet scheme for buying and selling gold coins, and that he might have manipulated or threatened his

son-in-law into taking the fall for him when the plan
went bad?

Or maybe, as Maude suggested, Leo White had emptied his coffers to leave the country. And maybe he
hadn't intended to leave alone. Maybe Sandy Lanier had
used her yearly hiking trip as a cover for her plan to run
away with her married lover.

And maybe I was wrong about all of it.

All I knew for sure was that Sandy Lanier was somehow connected to two people who had died violent
deaths within the past week, and now she was missing.
And this time I didn't have anyone else to turn to. I had
to take care of this one by myself.

Maude was minding the kennel when I arrived to drop
off Ringo. She recognized him immediately and lost no
time bustling him into a warm bath, a meal and a dry
kennel. While I snatched up my search and rescue supplies, she gave me a brief and encouraging report on
Uncle Roe. I ignored the nagging little voice inside that
reminded me how many rules I was breaking by not
sharing my information with the authorities, and concentrated instead on how important it was that my uncle not
be exposed to stress from the office. Besides, it wasn't
information that I had as much as it was speculation. I
wasn't even sure, as Rick had repeatedly reminded me,
that Sandy was in trouble.

"But I *am* sure," I told Maude, swinging my pack over
my shoulder. "Rick says she could have just changed her
mind about hiking, but you know as well I as do she

wouldn't just leave Ringo out in the woods. Something had to have happened."

"That would appear likely," agreed Maude. "But I don't know what you think you can do about it this afternoon. It's been three days, with a rainstorm in between, and you don't even know where to start."

"Where to start is exactly what I hope to find out," I said. "I know Cisco can't track Sandy. But he *can* track Ringo backward from the place he was found at the campsite. I don't know how far we'll get before we lose the trail, but all I can do is try. And maybe, with luck, I'll find something that will convince Rick to put together a full-fledged search."

Maude screwed tight the lid on a thermos of coffee and tucked it into my pack as I headed for the door. "Good luck," she said. "And for God's sake, be careful."

"Routine," I called back to her, and raced across the yard to join Cisco, who was already waiting in the truck.

What Rick referred to as "Campsite Number Three" was one of the lower campsites in what we called a primitive area—that meant no toilets, no showers, no RV hookups and no tent pads. There were concrete picnic tables and a trash can near the road, and that was where I parked. From there, through the nearly naked branches of trees, I could see the glint of the lake at the bottom of the hill in the distance.

Cisco was trained to track human scent, and when he put on his tracking harness and SAR vest, that was what he did—for the most part. But, being a dog, he would also track whatever scent caught his super-sensitive nose, and was just stubborn enough to follow that scent until he either found the source or lost the trail. Some of his favorite things to track were deer, rabbits and other dogs. Naturally this unfortunate tendency to go off on tangents was something we tried to discourage in tracking class. Today, however, I was counting on it.

Because I didn't want to confuse him, I didn't put on his vest or harness. I snapped a light lead on him until we were away from the road, and let him sniff eagerly around the picnic tables. I could tell—I really could—by the way he held his ears and waved his tail that what he was now excited about was another dog, not a person. When he bounded off through the woods, I was positive of it.

The forest floor was damp, but that was good; it would hold the scent better. The cool air, deep in the canopy of the woods, would pool the scent close to the ground as well, hopefully concentrating it into something Cisco could easily recognize and categorize. He worked a zigzag pattern in a happy, springing gait, occasionally looking back at me to see whether I was following. When he saw me close, he would pounce off again as though hardly able to believe his luck. Usually when I followed him on one of his wild goose—or wild deer, dog or rabbit—chases through the woods, I was red-faced and angry, shouting for him to come back to me that very minute. This, for Cisco, was a day out of school.

As we moved downhill toward the lake, we left forest service land and moved into the wildlife management area. "Wildlife management" is not to be confused with "wildlife preserve." In a wildlife management area, hunting is not only permitted but encouraged. Several dirt roads crossed the wooded area, and on one of them I saw a familiar black Range Rover parked. The vanity plate on the back read YOUNG1. Very cute. Wouldn't you know that, a dozen miles from nowhere, the one person who would be sharing the woods with me would be a flatlander fool pretending to hunt.

I called Cisco to me and snapped on his lead.

It occurred to me that the road intersected with the lake trail about a hundred yards to the east. It was not entirely out of the question that Sandy might have decided to hike down to the lake . . . especially if she had a lover who had rented a cabin there.

I had not said anything about Leo White's death to her, only Mickey's. She might not have known that he was dead. She might have assumed that whatever plan they had made was still on. My mind balked at imagining that pretty, vivacious, dog-loving woman at the center of such a cold-blooded plot. In fact, I simply couldn't do it. But Cisco *had* tracked Ringo this far.

Maybe it was a long shot, but I took Cisco down the dirt road until I spied the lake trail, littered with leaves and almost indistinguishable, curving off into the woods. I unleashed my dog.

Cisco galloped down the trail, occasionally sniffing the ground but giving no sign that he was finding anything of particular interest. Accustomed to being on the twenty-foot tracking lead, he rarely got more than fifteen or twenty feet ahead of me, and checked back regularly to make sure I was still there. But he gave absolutely no signs that he was on the trail of anything more fascinating than the occasional squirrel or raccoon who had darted up a tree sometime within the past hour or so.

I was about to call him and start back toward the dirt road when Cisco, perhaps fifteen feet ahead of me, suddenly skidded to a stop, ears and tail forward, and barked. It was a startled bark, as though he had seen or heard something unexpected in the woods, and I stopped still, looking around alertly.

In the sudden silence of a still autumn afternoon I could hear a leaf dislodge itself from a branch and float to the ground, brushing the passing leaves with a crinkling sound. And then I could hear something else—a sudden movement in the brush, sliding leaves and rattling branches, sticks cracking underfoot.

I called out, "Sandy?"

I turned around slowly, shading my eyes against the low-lying sun. "Sandy!"

Suddenly Cisco barked again, his greeting bark, his excited bark, and he dashed forward into the woods.

I cried, "Cisco!" and ran after him, but too late.

There was the crack of a gunshot, the high-pitched yelp of an animal in pain, and my world came to an end.

Chapter Fourteen

I remember screaming, a hoarse, inarticulate, terrified *"Noooo!"* I remember plunging down the trail, skidding, falling, scrambling up again before I hit the ground, splashing across a ditch, into the woods, falling to my knees beside my dog, who lay on his side, his eyes rolled back in his head, his beautiful golden fur dark and wet with blood.

I tried to stroke him but my hands were shaking convulsively. Strange sounds were coming out of my throat. I tore off my backpack, emptied it on the ground, pawed through it for the first aid kit, tried to think. Breathing, bleeding . . . I couldn't remember the third "b" of the first aid protocol. I couldn't remember the right order. I didn't think he was breathing. I couldn't get the first aid kit open. All I could do was kneel there with my hands cupping his sweet, still head, shaking and making choking noises that sounded like, "OhGodohGodohGod . . ."

There was a crashing sound, a man's voice: "Are you all right? What happened?"

I whirled around, and there was Miles Young, in his ridiculous L.L.Bean canvas hunting pants and plaid jacket, deer rifle slung over his shoulder, stepping high to avoid the ditch as he came toward me. In a blur of fury I flung myself on him, screaming, "You shot my dog, you stupid son of a bitch! You shot Cisco! You shot him!" I was pounding at him with my fists, wasting precious energy, trying to get his face, his eyes, roaring at him inarticulately.

He caught my arms and shoved me away from him, his gaze going over my shoulder first in puzzlement, then swiftly darkening in concern. I tried to wrench away from him and he gave me a little shake. "Is he alive?" he asked in a voice that sounded too cold, too calm.

I gasped, "I don't know." And with those words all the fight went out of me, and I had no more time to spare for rage. I pulled away from Miles and went back to my dog.

A fierce calm seized me, a clear level-headedness. I placed my hand on Cisco's chest and felt his shallow breathing. My hand came away wet and red. I found the roll of gauze in my first aid kit and quickly unrolled a wad, improvising a pressure bandage for the gaping wound I could see in his shoulder. I shook out the silvery space blanket and tried to get it around him, but it was slippery and hard to manage. I knew I couldn't carry him like that.

I was barely aware of Miles Young standing over me until I said out loud, breathlessly, "It's okay, boy, hold on, sweetie, I'm going to get you back to town."

Miles dropped down beside me, holding out his red

plaid jacket. "Wrap him in this," he commanded. "I'll carry him to my car."

I hesitated, but for not even a second. Gently I secured Cisco's muzzle closed with another strip of gauze, because even the sweetest dog will snap when disoriented and in pain, and tucked the heavy jacket under and around him. Cisco didn't even whimper as Miles Young lifted him in his arms.

I don't remember the trip down the mountain. I sat in the backseat of Miles's Range Rover with Cisco's head in my lap, mechanically giving directions to Doc Withers's place, never taking my eyes off my sweet boy. It was close to dusk when we pulled up in front of the clinic, and they were getting ready to close up. But when Ethel saw me tumble out of the strange vehicle, covered in blood, the whole family rushed out to help. Doc was the only one who realized immediately that the blood was not mine, and he brought a veterinary stretcher.

I wanted to go into the surgery with them, but Ethel firmly closed the door against me. I knew she had dealt with hundreds of hysterical clients over the years and she was probably right, but I had never expected to be treated like a hysterical client. I had never expected to *be* one.

After what seemed like a lifetime, Crystal came out and sat on the hard wooden bench beside me. She said, "Daddy said to tell you he's giving him oxygen and blood, and X-raying the shoulder, but he doesn't think the bullet hit an organ. Mama said I was to go up to the house and get you a Coke or something. What do you want?"

I shook my head. My hands were clasped firmly between my knees to keep them from shaking, and I tried not to rock back and forth. That would make me look hysterical. "Nothing, thanks. I'm fine. I think I should be in there with him. Cisco would be calmer if I was there."

She said, "Daddy's already put him under for the X-Ray. He wouldn't even know you."

She stood up awkwardly. "Well, if you don't want anything . . ."

Again I shook my head.

She nodded toward Miles Young, who stood beside the door, talking softly on his cell. I hated him. I had never hated anyone so much. "What about your friend?" she asked.

"No." It was hard to speak through all that hate. "Just let me know what the X-ray shows, okay?"

"Okay."

As she went back into the inner sanctum, Miles flipped his phone closed and came over to me. "Listen," he said, "I can have a helicopter here in fifteen minutes to fly you to Clemson or the University of Georgia, two of the best veterinary hospitals in the southeast. You can even take your own vet along to watch him during the flight. Just say the word."

I stared at him. "You think that makes it okay? Do you *really* think that makes it okay?" I couldn't stand to look at him, and I jerked my head away. Then I couldn't stand not to look at him, and I turned back. My voice was low and tight and much steadier than I would have thought possible. "I knew something like this was going to happen. From the first day I saw you, bumbling around in the woods with your idiot friends playing Big White Hunter, shooting at anything that moves . . . You wouldn't know a deer if it jumped through your windshield, and you think you can just go out and roam the woods with a deadly weapon . . . He was a therapy dog! He saved lives! He—"

I caught myself suddenly with a broken sob that choked in my throat, and pressed both hands to my lips to prevent it from escaping. I had said *was*. I had talked about my dog in the past tense.

Miles Young looked down at me gravely. He said quietly, "I'm only going to say this once. I was a marksman in the Gulf War. I've been hunting since I was twelve years old. If I sight a deer, I bag a deer. And I did not fire my rifle today."

I closed my eyes. I whispered, "He was learning how to dance."

And because I knew if I sat there another minute I would burst into tears, and if I started crying I would never stop, I got up and walked outside. I stayed there, letting the cold wrap itself around me and the blue mountain shadows drape themselves over me, until Crystal opened the door of the clinic and told me her dad was taking Cisco into surgery.

Miles did not leave. I didn't know why he stayed, but he sat there on one of the two wooden captain's chairs that, along with the bench upon which I sat, furnished the waiting room, and he drank the coffee that Crystal provided from a paper cup. He didn't try to talk to me. I gave him credit for that.

Less than an hour later, the door opened, and Buck came in. Miles got to his feet, regarding the uniform Buck wore with interest, but he said nothing. I stayed where I was, staring up at him. "Who called you?"

"Crystal."

She would.

He said, tight faced, "What happened?"

I tipped my head toward Miles. "Hunting accident. He shot Cisco."

Miles stepped forward and extended his hand. "Officer," he said, "I'm Miles Young. And I'm afraid she's mistaken. I was packing up for the day when I heard the shot."

Buck looked at his hand but did not shake it. He turned back to me. "How is he?"

"In surgery."

At that moment the door to the surgery opened and Doc came out. I jumped to my feet, but before I could speak he said, "He's going to be fine. Bullet lodged in the muscle, not the bone. Nicked an artery, but you did right with the pressure bandage, kept him from losing too much blood. He'll limp for a while, but I don't see why he shouldn't be running through the woods again in no time. He can go home tomorrow, if he does okay tonight."

He reached into the pocket of his lab coat and brought out a capped vial. "Here's the bullet."

Buck took it from him. He looked at Miles. "Do you mind if I have a look at your weapon, sir?"

Miles looked at the vial, and he replied mildly, "Not at all."

They headed toward the door, and I said to Doc, "I want to see him. I want to sit with him."

He knew better than to try to stop me that time.

I sat on the concrete floor by the open door of the kennel, my hand resting on the cool fur that covered Cisco's hip. He looked shrunken, like a stuffed toy, and even his fur didn't look real—it was dry and lifeless and stuck up in all different directions, like it had been glued on. Above and below the long line of black stitches on his shoulder, the fur had been shaved bare from neck to midriff, and it looked pathetic. He was still deeply unconscious from the anesthesia, but he knew I was there. I was certain of it.

The door at the end of the corridor opened, and I knew from the sound of the footsteps that it was Buck who entered. He squatted down beside me, smelling of cold outdoors and gun oil—two scents I would always associate with Buck. Tonight they brought me no comfort.

I said tightly, without looking at him, "Where's Wyn?" I knew I should have regretted the words the minute I spoke them, but I did not. I was filled with rage, filled with hate. I had not yet come to realize that the person I hated was myself. I repeated, "Where's your partner?"

A brief silence, then he said, "Off duty."

I still didn't look at him. I stroked Cisco's dull, lifeless fur, and willed him to know I was there.

Buck said, "You owe Mr. Young an apology. He didn't shoot Cisco."

Now I looked at him, sharply. "Of course he did. He's an idiot. He shouldn't be allowed to own a gun. He—"

"He was carrying a deer rifle," Buck interrupted, "and that's all. The bullet Doc took out of Cisco's shoulder belonged to a forty-five caliber handgun."

I stared at him, and Buck said, "Look for yourself." He opened the vial and tipped the bullet into my hand. I felt an immediate repulsion for the cool metal against my skin, and I quickly returned the bullet to him. But he was right. It had come from a handgun, not a rifle.

My head was fuzzy. It didn't make sense. "Who hunts with a forty-five? What were they doing out in the woods with a handgun?"

Buck said, "I had some boys go check out the place where it happened. Guess you didn't realize how close you were to the lake, to the cabin where Mickey White was found." His steady gaze held mine. "The police tape had been broken. Somebody had been in there. The place was trashed. So why don't you tell me what you were doing up on the lake trail this afternoon?"

He sounded so officious, so calm and in control and just-this-side-of-TV-cop that I think, at that moment, something snapped inside me. I said, low in my throat, "You don't get to talk to me like that." I turned on him. "You're not my uncle. You're not even my husband. You're for damn sure not the sheriff, and you don't get to talk to me like that! Where were *you*? Why weren't you there when I needed you? This never would have happened if you'd been there, damn it, Buck, you're supposed to be there!"

I couldn't believe it. My nose was running, my face was wet and my throat was filled with mucus. Before I knew it his arm was around me, and I was sobbing against his shoulder. It was painful weeping, the kind that stabbed behind my eyes and robbed my breath and made ugly choking sounds come from my chest. He held me tight against him, with one hand pressing into the back of my skull, until I exhausted myself with the force of it.

As I lay hiccuping against him, he said softly. "Ah, baby. Hell of a week for you, huh? I'm sorry for my part in it."

I squeezed my eyes tightly closed. "You're my best friend, Buck. Do you know how bad it feels to hate your best friend? I can't stand to think about losing you."

He took my face in both his hands, and he moved me away from him, so that he could look into my eyes. His own eyes were dark and serious. He said, "I'll always be your friend. I'll always be here for you. Listen to me, and believe that." His fingers tightened briefly on my face, as though to press the truth of his words into my brain, and then relaxed.

He pushed back my hair, and his eyes followed the path of his hands, tracing over my face as though memorizing it. He said softly, but steadily, "We have some papers to sign, okay? We've got some growing up to do, some things to face. But between us, it's okay. I'll always be there for you, Rainey. I'll always be your friend."

I tried to draw in a deep breath, hiccuped and nodded. He pulled out a handkerchief. I blew my nose.

He said, "What happened up there?"

So I told him about Sandy Lanier, about Letty Cranston's phone call and the affair that Leo White had had, and how David Kines had threatened to have Leo killed. I told him how Sandy had reacted when she met Hero and learned of Mickey's death, and about Ringo showing up, lost and alone, at the campsite. I even told him about my call to David Kines.

To someone else, his expression might have been impassive. But I recognized the tight, grim lines that bracketed his mouth when I was finished.

He said, "I'll put out an all-points for Sandy Lanier. Don't worry. If she's still around here, we'll find her."

He reached past me and laid his hand on Cisco's chest. He kept it there for a long moment, in quiet affection, and then he straightened up. "Come on. I'll give you a ride home."

I shook my head. "I'm staying. Ethel will bring me a cot or something. I'm not leaving him."

He did not seem surprised. "Where's your car? I'll have one of the boys bring it by here for you before morning."

I told him, and he stood. "I'll take care of it," he said, and I knew he would.

He turned his gaze toward the kennel where Cisco lay, and his expression softened. "Get better, big guy," he said.

I watched him go, but I didn't speak until the door had

closed behind him. And then all I said was a very soft, "Good-bye, Buck."

I turned to Cisco, entwining my fingers in his fur, and there I stayed until morning, until his wet, licking kisses nudged me to wakefulness.

Chapter Fifteen

"We have a lost dog here by the name of Ringo, brown and white, picked up day before yesterday on the Old Forest Service Road. I understand his owner's name is Sandy. So, Sandy, if you're listening out there, how about giving us a call at the radio station, or stop by Dog Daze Boarding and Training Center off of County Road 16. Raine Stockton is taking good care of him, but your pup wants to go home.

"Funeral Services for Ima Lee Tucker will be held tomorrow afternoon at two at Calvary Baptist Church. Visitation tonight from six to eight at Sutter's Funeral Home. The family requests—"

I snapped off the radio. The station had been faithful about announcing Ringo's whereabouts at the top of the hour, every hour. If Sandy had access to a radio, she knew where her dog was. But it was beginning to seem less and less likely that she would do anything about it—either because she couldn't, or because she didn't want to.

And I simply couldn't believe that I had misjudged her that badly.

Buck had confirmed that Sandy Lanier had, in fact, been Mickey White's physical therapist. He had tracked down her vehicle registration and had a lookout for her car, but that was all I knew about the investigation. It was, in fact, all I wanted to know.

No one had to point out my error in judgment in taking matters into my own hands instead of turning over my information to the authorities. The consequences of my foolishness gazed at me with sweet, forgiving eyes from his plush dog bed in the quiet storeroom that opened off the office. Occasionally he would entertain himself by chewing on a Nylabone or licking the cheese out of a rubber Kong toy. He took lots of naps, and got an abundance of petting and as many treats as the vet would allow. Sonny said—and I had no reason to dispute this—that in Cisco's opinion, this was the best time of his life.

In truth, dogs recover from major traumas like illness and surgery with a great deal more aplomb than people do. Some think it's because they process pain differently, and others believe it's because dogs don't worry themselves to death, as people tend to do. All I know is that my biggest struggle was in keeping Cisco quiet and resting, instead of bouncing up and down the stairs and wrestling with the other dogs. It was for that reason that I had installed him in the storage room, safely behind a baby gate, close enough so that he could see me and I could stop by and pet him every few minutes, but out of the center of traffic and, hopefully, away from anything that would excite him.

"Are you sure you don't mind doing this?" I asked Maude as she pulled on her coat and her lightweight driving gloves.

"Not a bit of it. I'll enjoy the drive, and it's been ages since I've seen Katie. Not since her wedding, in fact."

My cousin Kate was flying in that afternoon with plans to stay for a couple of weeks to help out Aunt Mart after Uncle Roe was released from the hospital. Naturally, I couldn't bear to leave Cisco, even for the few hours it would take to pick Kate up from the Asheville airport and return. But even if it had not been for Cisco, I couldn't have left the kennel. Wes Richards was coming by in less than an hour to evaluate Hero, and I had to be here.

"We'll stop by the hospital first," Maude said, "and then we'll go get a bite to eat before I settle her in at home. Are you sure you don't want to meet us in town?"

I glanced over my shoulder at Cisco and she smiled. "Never mind. I'll see you in the morning, then."

She opened the door, and then turned back. "Oh, and don't try to move that kerosene by yourself. I'll help you load it on the dolly in the morning and get it over to the shed."

Every October we ordered a fifty-gallon drum of kerosene to use in the emergency kennel heaters in case of a power outage. And every year the delivery man dropped it off in front of the kennel instead of taking it to the storage shed fifty feet away as we repeatedly asked him to do.

"Don't worry," I said. I reached down to absently stroke Hero's ear. "As soon as Wes Richards leaves I'm going to clean up some paperwork and call it a day. I feel like I could sleep for about a week."

"Probably wouldn't hurt you a bit," she said.

Cisco and Hero seemed to have come to a détente, probably because, from Cisco's point of view, there was absolutely no doubt who was Best Dog around here, and it was himself. Cisco seemed to have no problem with Hero keeping me company in the office, nor did he object when Hero shared his space in the storeroom, where a spare crate was set up. After all, it was Cisco who was lying on an orthopedic dog bed with his own personal water dish embossed with silver pawprints so close that he only had to stretch out his neck to drink from it, surrounded by toys and gourmet munchies. He probably felt he could spare a little pity for the visiting dog.

I spent some time reviewing Hero's commands, but it was a halfhearted effort that brought me little pleasure. Hero was a great dog, but Buck had been right when he called me a groupie. I always wanted bigger and better; I always expected more. I had forgotten that I already had a hero, and his name was Cisco.

Over and over in the past two days I had replayed the details of the incident in my mind, and tried to make it match what Buck had told me. Someone had invaded the cabin that Mickey and Leo White had rented, and had trashed it. It didn't take much imagination to assume they were looking for something, and that the something they were looking for might have been a bag full of gold coins.

Then along I come, thrashing through the woods, getting much too close, making far too much noise . . . had the shot been meant for me? Cisco had seen something in the woods that startled him, and he had lunged for it. In doing so, had he saved my life?

If this were one of those television cop shows that my aunt liked to watch, there would be a manhunt in force right now, roadblocks would be in place, forensic investigators would be working all sorts of miracles, and within twenty-four hours the killer of Mickey White would be behind bars with an unbreakable chain of evidence and the case would be solved. In real life, in a small town in the Smoky Mountains, things are a little messier—and a lot slower. The person who had shot Cisco was still at large. And so was Mickey White's murderer.

And there wasn't a damn thing I could do about either one.

Wes Richards arrived right on time in a white van with COASTAL ASSISTANCE DOGS stenciled on the doors in red letters. I gently closed the door to the storage room where Cisco was napping, and went out to meet him.

He was much younger than I had expected. He shook my hand firmly, thanked me profusely for what I had done for Hero and accepted my offer of a cup of coffee. Maude had made the coffee, not I, and the fact that he drank it stoically, without complaint, raised him quite a few notches in my regard.

We talked for a few minutes about Hero and about
dogs in general. I told him that Leo White's body had
been found, and he replied that he had already learned as
much from Mickey's father.

"So there's no relative who's able to take the dog?" I
asked.

"No," he said. "But that's not a problem. If Nero is not
able to be reassigned, we have a long list of families who
would love to adopt a young, highly trained dog like
him."

I smiled weakly. "I'm sure." I stood. "I guess you'd
like to see him."

I must say I was impressed with the way Wes, despite his youth, was transformed once he took Hero's
lead. He became a dog handler: confident, assured, firm
but fair, leaving no doubt in Hero's mind or anyone
else's what he expected from the dog at any given moment. As he worked with Hero, he explained to me a
little about the training program, and the reasoning behind each of the sixty-eight basic commands all of their
dogs were taught before they were considered suitable
for placement as service dogs.

Hero performed magnificently, of course. He brought
Wes's car keys, which he had dropped in the trash can, to
the chair in which Wes was sitting. He put his front paws
on my desk and retrieved a memo pad. He went quietly
to a corner and lay down when Wes commanded him to
do so. I knew all of this was just child's play for him, and
that Wes was letting him practice the easy commands
only so that he would feel comfortable.

Then Wes put him in a down-stay, walked behind

him and dropped a stack of heavy books onto the concrete floor. They made a sound like rapid gunfire. Hero
whirled around, barking, then charged toward the door
with his ears back and his tail down. I caught his collar.
"Easy boy," I said softly. "Calm down."

Hero pressed himself against my leg, tail still tucked.

Wes came over to me, his face impassive, and took
Hero's collar. He calmly returned the dog to the exact
same spot where he had broken his down-stay, which I
knew perfectly well was the correct procedure, and he
repeated the experiment. He repeated it several times,
with steadily worsening results. When it became clear
that the dog's distress was nearing critical level, he
snapped on the lead, asked Hero to sit, and then
praised him gently. He released the dog to follow his
instincts, and Hero's instincts were to hide behind my
desk.

Wes Richards looked at me with deep regret in his
eyes. "He was such a great dog," he said.

"So that's it? He's out of the program?"

He said, "It can take up to two years to train a service
dog, and our waiting list is three years old. As valuable
as Nero is to us, his chances of rehabilitation are so slim,
and the time factor is so crucial, that I just can't take
trainers away from dogs who have a real chance of success." He drew a breath and shook his head. "I hate this,"
he said.

Then he picked up Nero's lead and extended his hand.
"I can't thank you enough for taking care of him. I can
tell you went above and beyond the call of duty with
him."

"You're not driving back this afternoon, are you?"

"Actually, I'd planned to stay over and get an early start in the morning."

"I'll keep Hero overnight for you if you like," I volunteered quickly.

"Thanks," he said, smiling. "I hated to ask you to do more than you've already done, but I'm frankly not sure what the pet policy of the hotel is where I'm staying, and it would be a big help if I could pick him up in the morning."

I walked him to the door. "It's no trouble at all. As you've probably guessed, I've grown pretty fond of him." Then I said thoughtfully, "I know you've got a waiting list, but do you ever . . . that is, would you consider adopting Hero to someone who's *not* on the list?"

He looked surprised, but also hopeful. "Do you mean you?"

I shook my head. "No. I'd love to have him, but I can't. I was thinking about someone else."

"Well, there would be a lot of factors to consider. We'd have to do an interview and a home visit. Could you tell me something about the person you have in mind?"

"In the morning," I promised him. "I have to make a phone call, check some things out . . ."

As soon as he drove away, I hurried back to the desk. "Hero," I excitedly told the huddled mass of insecurity under my desk, "I don't know why I didn't think of this before! It's the perfect solution for everybody. And the best part is, you don't have to leave. I can visit you any-time I want."

I scooted behind the desk and picked up the phone. But I had dialed only three digits when the door opened on a gust of cold air. I looked up and dropped the phone back into its cradle as Sandy Lanier walked in.

Chapter Sixteen

My impression of Sandy had been that she was a pretty woman—even beautiful, with her long blond hair and her flowing gold-and-white top. But she didn't look pretty now. Her hair was pulled back severely from her face and caught at the nape of her neck, and it looked dull and dry. She wore oversized dark glasses and no makeup, and her lips were chapped and cracked. The sage green hiking parka that she wore was stained and torn at the elbow, and her jeans were baggy and thread-bare.

She was accompanied by a man in a black leather jacket with zippered pockets, pencil-legged jeans and boots. He had scraggly dark hair that was a little too long and wore aviator sunglasses. He hung back at the door as Sandy came forward.

I said, in a stunned tone, "Sandy?"

"Hi," she replied. Her smile seemed tight, as though it hurt her mouth. "I heard on the radio that you have my dog—that my dog Ringo was found, and that you have him here. Is that right? Is he okay?"

There was genuine concern in her voice with the last and I hastened to assure her, "Yes, I have him, he's fine. But we've all been worried about you. I thought something had happened—"

The man stepped forward impatiently. "Can we just get the dog and go?"

Sandy said, "Raine, this is my boyfriend, Alan. We were camping and Ringo got away from us the other morning. He's such a silly dog." Her voice sounded high and artificial. "He never learned to come when I call. He probably shouldn't even be allowed off leash. It was all my fault. I hope he didn't cause you too much trouble."

I stared at her, remembering the perfectly heeling dog who had never left her side, had never needed a leash even in the midst of throngs of people and children with hot dogs and ice cream cones. Why was she lying? What was wrong with her?

And in a sudden surge of cold anger I said, "I thought you were hurt. Cisco and I were searching for you, and somebody shot him."

I thought I saw her flinch, but it was difficult to tell underneath the big glasses. She wet her pale, cracked lips. "How—awful."

The man—Alan, she had called him—said, "We're in kind of a hurry, so if you could just get the dog—"

I had been dimly aware of a low rumbling at my feet, but with everything else that was racing through my mind I didn't recognize the sound for what it was. When the stranger moved toward the desk, however, the throaty growl suddenly erupted into a furious, snarling, barking frenzy as Hero leapt over my desk, toenails scrabbling, teeth bared, and charged.

Sandy gave a cry of alarm and shrank back, the man swore and raised his arm to guard his face and I instinctively grabbed Hero's collar, dragging him back. Without a word, I swept the snarling, barking, lunging dog into the storeroom, maneuvered him into a crate, and shot the bolt. Cisco tried to struggle to his feet, excited by all the noise, and I told him sharply, "Down! Stay!"

Looking disappointed, he obeyed, and I quickly closed the storeroom door behind me.

"I am so sorry!" I said. My heart was pounding with adrenaline, and my voice was a little breathless. "I don't know what got into him!"

"What kind of place are you running here, anyway, lady?" demanded the man angrily. "Goddamn dog almost bit me. I hope your insurance is paid up. You call this a dog school?"

"I'm sorry. He's usually so friendly. . . ." Flustered, I bent down to pick up the papers Hero had dislodged from my desk, and that was when I noticed the man's boots.

A snake came, and then she died.

The boots were snakeskin. From my point of view near the floor, from a dog's point of view, the diamondback pattern was unmistakable.

A flash of unwanted certainty hit me and froze me, for a fraction of a second, in place. It was Sandy, after all. Sandy and this snakeskin-wearing man she called her boyfriend who had killed Mickey White and possibly her husband, who had trashed her cabin looking for the coins, who had shot Cisco when we got too close. I felt it in my gut like a punch in the stomach, and then logic reestablished itself.

It was absurd, ridiculous. There was absolutely no reason to think Sandy was involved at all. Just because she happened to have been the dead woman's physical therapist meant nothing, less than nothing. There was no evidence that she had even been in town when Mickey White was murdered. Just because she had disappeared right before the cabin was ransacked, just because Cisco had been shot while searching for her . . .

Watch out for snakes. . . .

It was impossible. Sandy Lanier was a dog lover. And dog lovers didn't kill people.

Well, maybe they did. But they never risked the safety of their dogs in the process.

I straightened up slowly, clutching a handful of papers, and tried not to stare at the man. My heart couldn't seem to find its normal rhythm, and my breath came shallowly, too quickly.

Sandy was saying, "Please, could I just get Ringo? I want to see him." There was no mistaking the note of desperation in her voice.

"Sure." I turned quickly and went behind the desk. "He's in back. I'll get him. I would have kept him in the house, but I've had a crisis or two myself over the past couple of days. It seemed best to keep him in the kennel." I was babbling. I hoped no one noticed. "I'm glad you're okay. I was afraid something had happened." Obviously something had happened. The only question was *what*.

"I want to pay you, of course." Sandy was fumbling in her purse. She took out a checkbook.

"No, it's not necessary." Snakeskin boots. Lots of people had them. They meant nothing. I had nothing to go on but Sonny's interpretation of what a dog had told her and even that did not prove anything. *Watch out for snakes. . . .* "I do this. I mean, rescue dogs, that's what I do. There's no charge for boarding rescues."

"Please, I insist." Her voice was tight, and she scribbled out a check.

"Really, it's—"

She thrust the check into my hand. "Take it," she said, and something about her tone, about the determined way she held the check out to me, made me take it from her and glance at it.

On the PAY TO line she had written in block letters: *HELP ME*. Underneath it, in the IN THE AMOUNT OF area, she had written another word, and underscored it. The word was <u>*Gun*</u>.

I realized I was staring at the check. When I looked at her, I was sure that everything I knew was written on my face, and that the man could see it. I cleared my throat, folded the check into my hand with what I hoped was a casual gesture, and plucked the cordless phone off the desk. I turned toward the door that led to the kennels. "I'll just go get him."

The man took a step forward. "What do you need the phone for?" he demanded.

I turned to him, trying to appear cool and in control.

Trying to look normal. I was certain he could see the pounding of my heart, the shaking of my hands. I said, "We don't have an extension in the back. I always take the phone."

He said, "We'll answer it if it rings."

I almost managed a smile. "Oh, I couldn't let you do that."

He took a step toward me. There was menace in his eyes, in his posture. "Leave the phone."

I cut my eyes toward the kennel door, wondering what my chances were of making it to the other side of the door, locking it, and dialing 911 before he could stop me. I was only inches away. I stretched my fingers toward the door handle, and that was my big mistake. He lunged toward me and the kennel door and was on me before I could turn the handle. Sandy screamed and tore at him. He sent her sprawling against a display of leashes. The metal rack came down with a crashing sound as he wrestled the phone from me, tossing it across the room. I tried to claw at his eyes, but he punched me in the stomach hard enough to knock the breath out of me.

"Bitch!" he shouted. "You cheap, lying whore!"

It was only when he turned to push Sandy back against the wall that I realized he was shouting at her, not me. I was gasping for breath like a beached fish, my vision was blurring and terror started to fill my lungs where air should have been. Distantly, I heard barking. Cisco? Hero?

"What did you do? What the fuck did you do?" The check had fallen from my clenched fist in the struggle, and he snatched it up, read it, tossed it down. "You never

knew where the money was! It was a trick to get me
here! You lying—"

The air returned to my lungs in a whoop and I charged
at him head down, just as he drew back to hit Sandy
again. All I did was knock him off balance, and before I
could dive for the phone—which is what I should have
done in the first place—he grabbed me by the neck and
tossed me against Sandy. We fell in a pile on the floor,
and when I looked again, it was into the ugly maw of a
.45 caliber pistol.

He grabbed one of the leashes and tossed it to me. His
face was covered with a fine sheen of sweat and he was
breathing hard. "Tie her hands together," he commanded.
"Do it right. I'm watching."

Now that her glasses had been knocked away, I could
see that both of Sandy's eyes were blackened and that her
right one was swollen almost shut. I felt a stab of remorse
for what I had secretly accused her of, and a swell of relief that I had been wrong. Neither of those emotions
were helpful now, though, as my brain raced helplessly,
foolishly, to try to think of some way to overpower or out-
smart the gunman.

"Tighter!" he commanded, jerking the gun at me, and
I tightened the binding until Sandy gasped in pain.

"Sorry," I whispered.

If he had tossed me one of the expensive nylon or
leather leashes that had been on display, I would have
had a legitimate excuse to tie a poor knot—the half-inch
webbed nylon was too thick and the leather too slippery
to make a tight loop. But whether by accident or design

he had selected one of the cheap slip leads that was little more than coated rope. It made an excellent binding.

When her hands were tied, he grabbed me away from her and proceeded to bind my hands behind my back with the same force. I said, trying to distract him while I pushed my wrists as far apart as I could, "The police have the coins. They found them in the trunk of Leo White's car. This is not going to get you any closer to the money."

My uncle always said criminals were fundamentally stupid; otherwise, they wouldn't be criminals. My attempt to reason with him was a wasted effort. He pulled the knot so tight that I felt bones grind together, and I cried out.

"I'm sick of it," he said, breathing hard. "Sick of being lied to by you goddamn bitches. It's my goddamn money, and I'm getting it back, you hear?"

"You can't," I insisted. "You're already wanted for Mickey White's murder. The police are scouring the countryside—"

"I didn't kill her." He tied the knot hard and jerked me to my feet. "The stupid bitch offed herself, right there in front of me. The whole thing was her plan, her setup, her way of making sure her old man got what he deserved for stepping out on her. I brought her the gun. I was supposed to get the money. Half a million in gold coins for one little gun? Hell, yeah. I figured she was going to do her old man, yeah, but what did I care what she did with it? By that time I was going to be long gone.

"But that wasn't her plan at all, the lying bitch. She wanted to make it look like he murdered her, least that's what she told me when I got there. Called me stupid, said I'd been set up, and good luck collecting my fee, and then she blew her brains out, right there in front of me.

"But I ain't stupid. I knew my fingerprints were all over that gun. So I wiped it down and put her fingerprints back on the gun, but that's *all* I did. Nobody can say I murdered her. There's not a shred of evidence against me."

Except that you put the gun in the wrong hand, I thought, but didn't say. "Her husband must have come back while you were still there," I said. "He'd gone out for dog food but couldn't find the right brand. He saw his wife dead, saw you and ran. You chased him, but lost him in the dark, and he drove his car down a ravine."

"Shut up," he said. He opened the door that led to the kennels, and the muffled barking of the four dogs who were boarding there—including Ringo—was suddenly sharp and clear. He closed the door again.

"What about the dog?" I said quickly, trying now to do nothing more than buy time. "I don't understand how her service dog got locked outside the bedroom."

"I shut it out. I hate dogs, always have. White never would have known I was there if it hadn't been for that fool thing barking its head off. I could've got the money and got clean away."

He jerked Sandy to her feet and shoved her toward me. He nodded toward the storeroom door. "What's in there?" he demanded.

"Nothing. Dog food. Cleaning supplies."

He opened the door and shoved us inside. Hero started barking and lunging at the bars of his crate and Cisco started to push himself to his feet. I cried, "Cisco, no! Down!"

Looking a little ashamed of himself for forgetting his down-stay, Cisco sank back down to his bed.

The man leveled his gun at Hero's crate. "Make him shut up."

"I can't! I can't make a dog stop barking when he's scared!"

"I can."

"No!"

I flung all my weight upward and outward, into the man's shoulder. His gun arm jerked up and the shot, exploding in the small room, sounded like a cannon. Almost at the same moment I felt a stinging blow across the side of my head, and everything went dark.

A rough wet tongue across my eyes nudged me to consciousness. Feathery whiskers tickled my face. I tried to lift my hands to pet my dog but they were paralyzed. When I turned my head away, the pain of a thousand lightning bolts shot through it. I groaned and forced my eyes open. It was dark, but I came to understand that I was lying on my side on the cold concrete floor, and a heavy weight was preventing me from moving.

"Are you okay?"

The voice belonged to Sandy. Gradually my senses returned, as well as scraps of memory. Cisco's hot breath on my face was like a lifeline.

"Was I shot?" I whispered.

"No. Just knocked out. He hit you with the gun. Your head was bleeding. That's all I could see before he shut the door."

That explained why it was so dark. The room was concrete block, and windowless. I had left the overhead light off so that Cisco could rest.

I managed, through a sudden wave of nausea, "The dogs? Are they okay?"

"Yes. The bullet went into the ceiling, I think. Nero was just kind of huddled up in the crate. The gunshot really scared him."

I took a deep breath, careful not to move my head. "How long was I out?"

"A minute or two. He tied us together and locked the door. I haven't heard anything else."

I could feel her shoulder blades against mine, and when I tried to move my arms they were bound to my sides by what I gradually came to recognize as more leashes. It was hard to think. Cisco kept trying to lick my face. I just wanted to close my eyes and make the pain go away.

"Can you untie my hands?" I couldn't even feel my fingers.

"I've been trying. I can't reach them."

"Cisco," I said weakly, "lie down."

"He was very good," Sandy said. "He stayed on his bed the whole time. I think Alan forgot he was there."

Cisco gave a grunt as he lowered himself to the floor beside me. I felt his warm, heavy weight against my leg. I took a deep, slow breath, then another, trying to clear my head.

Sandy said brokenly, "I am so sorry. So sorry for dragging you into this."

I tried to think. Maude would not be back tonight. The kennel was within a half hour of closing and I didn't have any appointments. No one was expecting me anywhere, nor would anyone think anything other than I had gone to bed early if I didn't answer the phone. I could hear the muffled barking of the kennel dogs, but that wouldn't last long.

As my eyes adjusted to the dimness, I could make out the shape of shelves filled with dog food bags, covered bins of toys and clickers, bottles of spray disinfectant. No scissors, knives, box cutters or keys. No phone. All of those useful items were in the outer office.

I said, "Someone will be here in the morning. It might not be very comfortable tonight, but we'll be okay."

"I wish Ringo was here. Is he really okay?"

I said, "He's fine."

"Mesner was waiting for me when I left the Pet Fair Saturday afternoon. I had just put Ringo in the back of the car when he came out of nowhere and pushed me into the passenger seat. He drove my car up to that cabin—I guess it's the one Mickey and Leo had rented. There was police tape all around it. He made me get out, and steered my car into the lake. It was all I could do to get Ringo out before he did it. He was sure I knew where the money was. At first I denied it"—I remembered the bruises on her face—"and he tore the place apart looking for it. Then he thought it might be hidden out in the woods somewhere. He would leave me tied up while he looked for it. I guess . . . that's what happened the day you and Cisco came along."

I said, sounding stronger than I felt, "It wasn't your fault."

"After that, I knew he would kill me if I didn't give him some reason not to. So I told him he was right, I had the money and I would split it with him, but I wouldn't leave without Ringo. When I heard the announcement on the radio, it was like a godsend. I told him that I had the money in a safe deposit box back in Charleston and that I'd turn it over to him. But I wasn't leaving without my dog."

I said, "Is he really your boyfriend?"

"No." A broken sound of disgust. "God, no. He's some kind of hired gun of Mickey White's father. He tracked me down because of Leo. I was . . ." an unsteady breath. "Leo and I had an affair this summer. I broke it off after a few months, but he didn't want to let go. He kept e-mailing me, talking about us running away together. I kept trying to tell him it was over, but"—a shaky breath—"apparently he never got those e-mails. I think . . . from what I can tell, Mickey intercepted my e-mails to him, and changed them . . . made it look like I was setting up a rendezvous with him to leave the country. She knew I was coming up here; I had talked to her about it. She had it all worked out so that it would look like her husband killed her and ran away with me. She was a sad and twisted woman."

"Do you think she really killed herself, just like he said?"

She was silent for a moment. "She was in liver failure.

The doctors didn't expect her to live until Christmas. I don't think she told anyone. I only knew because I was on her treatment team at the hospital."

"I always wondered how the killer got past Hero," I said, "and how Hero got locked outside the bedroom. It was the one thing that didn't make sense. But if Mickey put him outside the room herself, in a down-stay, for example—"

"He would have stayed there," Sandy finished for me, "no matter what happened, until she released him."

"Only she never did," I said softly, and could barely think about how long the faithful dog had stayed there, waiting for his release command, until finally hunger, thirst and survival instinct had overridden his training, and he had begun to bark.

Suddenly I was brought back to the present, and I said sharply, "What's that smell?"

She hesitated. "It smells like some kind of chemical."

"No." A sudden dryness seized my throat, and the pounding of my heart sent lightning bolts through my brain. "It's kerosene."

Frantically I looked around. "If we try to stand up at the same time, we might be able to make it to the door. It has a turnbolt lock. I think I can move it with my shoulder."

"Our feet are tied together!"

"We've got to try."

Cisco got up with a worried whimper and limped to the door, sniffing at the bottom threshold.

"Oh, God," she said with a gasp. "I smell smoke!"

I braced my shoulders against hers and tried to get my

feet beneath me but collapsed almost immediately against an onslaught of fiery pain piercing my temples. Sandy struggled frantically to get her balance, crying, "He's set the place on fire! The dogs—Ringo! We've got to get out of here!"

With every movement there was a new explosion of pain in my head. Gray and white spots swam before my vision and I was drenched in a sudden cold sweat. A thick stickiness on the back of my neck suggested the wound had reopened.

"Wait!" I gasped. "Stop! I can't—"

"Ringo!" she said, half sobbing. "Oh, my God, Ringo!"

But she stopped struggling long enough for me to catch my breath, to slowly will the world back into focus. "The kennel is concrete block," I managed. "It won't burn. The dog doors are open to outside runs. They can get away from the smoke. They'll be okay."

If he hadn't closed the dog doors; if the dogs weren't too panicked or overcome by smoke to use them; if the bedding or the paper products we kept for cleaning didn't catch fire . . . We had to get out of here. The training rooms that adjoined the office had been fashioned from the original stable that had first inspired the idea for the kennel location, and they would go up like kindling. The concrete walls that separated that part of the building from this might delay the spread of the fire, but already enough oily smoke had seeped through the crack underneath the door to make my eyes water.

Hero stirred in his crate, rattling it. Cisco pawed worriedly at the door. The cool air of the storage room was sucking in the heated smoke from outside, now so thick I could taste it.

Think. Think.

Sandy started to cough. I tried to breathe shallowly.

Cisco pawed the door again. If I could get him to stand up on his back legs, he might accidentally hit the turnbolt with his paw and unlock the door. It was a desperate plan with virtually no chance for success, but I had no choice.

"Cisco," I called hoarsely. My throat convulsed and I tried not to cough. "Cisco, up!"

In the dimness, I could see him turn his head toward me. He started to come to me. "No!" I shouted. That time I did cough. "Up!"

He looked at the door. I actually thought he might do it. I sent up a silent prayer to the God of Dogs: *Please, please, please . . .*

It was the same prayer I had sent at every agility trial and obedience trial since Cisco had been competing, and my success rate was about fifty percent. But when a prayer is all you've got, a prayer is what you use.

Cisco sat in front of the door and whined. It took me a moment to realize that he was trying to stand up, but his shoulder wound prevented him. He needed his front legs to launch onto his back ones, and he had no use of the muscles in his right front leg.

He was trying, but he couldn't do it.

The smoke was thick now, and toxic. There was no way to pretend that it wouldn't kill us—all of us—long before the fire did.

Sandy gasped, "Can he tug?"

"What?"

"There's . . ." Coughing. "A rope . . ." More coughing. "Tied to the slide bolt on Nero's crate. I saw it . . .
before he locked us in here. Nero can . . ." Coughing.
"Can unlock doors. I've seen him."

"I know," I gasped. But what I was thinking, and
didn't want to waste the breath to say, was, *Oh my God!*
It was Mischief's crate that I had locked Hero into; Mischief, who had an annoying talent for unlocking the slide
bolt on her own crate, so I often had to tie it closed with
a piece of rope. If Cisco could release Hero from his
crate . . .

I called hoarsely, "Cisco, here."

Cisco came anxiously to me. "Cisco," I said, struggling to make the words audible. "Go kennel." He hesitated. He hated crates. He barely even recognized the
command. I repeated sternly, *"Go kennel."*

I was overcome by a fit of coughing. When I could
focus again, Cisco had wandered over to Hero's crate.
Thank you, thank you, God of Dogs. . . .

I choked, "Cisco, tug! *Tug!*"

And what I was thinking was, *I'll never ask you for
another double-Q, forget the utility dog title, please,
please, please, just tug, oh, please!*

And the next thing I knew, Hero was free from his
crate and sniffing the floor next to me. Sandy was making an odd sound that was part crying, part laughing, part
a triumphant, "Yes!"

My head spun. Smoke clogged my throat, cutting off
my oxygen, and I struggled to focus, to breathe. "Hero,"
I gasped. "Good dog. Go door. *Door.*"

He was not familiar with the environment, but he could see better in the dark than I could. He looked around, and he found the door. He jumped up and pawed the lock until it released, and the door opened outward against his weight onto a black tornado of smoke.

The smoke billowed inward like a tidal wave. I tried to speak, and what I wanted to do was to tell Hero to *run*, to save himself, to jump through a window if he had to and to take Cisco with him. My reason was fading, my head was spinning and black smoke burned my lungs. Whatever sounds I made were unintelligible.

Then I heard Sandy shouting, "Nero, phone! Find the phone!"

I couldn't breathe. My throat was closing up, my nose clogged with mucus. My lungs were bursting, ready to explode, and all I could taste in my mouth was oil and smoke. I felt Cisco's warm furry body pressed against mine. *Go!* I wanted to scream at him. *Go, don't stay here and die with me, go, run, be safe! Cisco, please go!*

But my precious dog didn't move.

And then, as though from far away, I heard a tinny, squawking voice: "Nine-one-one emergency. Do you have an emergency?"

I gasped, "Fire! Help—"

I thought I heard the voice reply, "Raine, is that you?" But mostly, all I heard was barking.

Chapter Seventeen

"You've got to admit," said Sonny, "it sounds like one of those stories that should be on Animal Planet. 'Miracle Dog Saves Woman from Certain Death.'"

I gave her a dry look. "Coming from the Woman Who Talks to Dogs," I said, "I guess that's saying a lot."

The doctors said I had sustained a concussion, in addition to smoke inhalation, and insisted on keeping me in the hospital overnight. Uncle Roe and I had been released from the hospital on the same day, and he hadn't stopped lecturing me yet.

My first few days at home had been shaky and uncertain, complicated by the repeated visits from law officers and insurance agents. But I was well on my way to recovery now, and to celebrate, Sonny had invited me to lunch at Miss Meg's, downtown Hansonville's most popular eatery.

She had also invited my cosurvivor, Sandy Lanier. To what I have to believe was the surprise of both of us, Sandy had accepted.

"I know it sounds miraculous," Sandy said, "but it's really just what Nero—I mean, Hero—was trained to do. The emergency button on Mickey's telephone was programmed to speed-dial nine-one-one—and so was Raine's. Most people's are. All Hero had to do was hit the button with his nose, just like he'd been trained to do at service dog school. Fortunately, you're set up with E–nine-one-one, so that the dispatcher knew where the call was coming from without your having to give her directions. Otherwise it might have been a different story altogether."

The volunteer fire department had arrived within ten minutes of the call. But long before that, sheriff's department deputies had pulled Sandy and me out of the kennel storeroom and onto the front lawn, where we were given oxygen and first aid by arriving paramedics.

The damage to the kennel had been slight, all things considered: mostly water and smoke. And no dogs had been harmed at all. However, getting the repairs done promised to be a lengthy and frustrating process, since every contractor in the county was tied up building Miles Young's house, and none of them was willing to take even a day off from such a lucrative project to bring in the equipment needed to do the cleanup on my little job.

My only clear memory of the events after the 911 call was of Buck, squeezing my fingers when they put me in the ambulance, the tenderness and the concern behind the bracing smile in his eyes as he said, "Damn, girl. When are you going to learn to stay out of trouble?"

He had sent yellow roses while I was in the hospital

even though he knew my favorite was yellow daisies, and he had signed the card from the whole department. But he had left word at the nurse's station that Cisco, a certified therapy dog, should be allowed to stay the night with me under the supervision of his competent handler, Maude Braselton. For that he was forgiven almost everything. Almost.

Sonny inquired gently of Sandy, "What will you do now?"

Sandy said quietly, "I had an affair with a married man. I screwed up my life."

She pushed salad around on her plate. So did I.

"I know it's no excuse," Sandy went on in a heavy voice, "but Mickey White was a bitter, unpleasant woman. She tormented poor Leo, and everyone else around her. People at the hospital dreaded the days she was scheduled to come in. I know she was in pain, and her frustration must have been tremendous, but she went out of her way to hurt and insult people. The spoiled rich kid who was so accustomed to having everything her way, and started throwing a permanent tantrum when she was diagnosed . . .

"Leo was just a decent guy doing the best he could for his disabled wife, and I guess I felt sorry for him at first. I would see him in the hospital coffee shop, and we would talk—or he would talk, mostly. He needed to unburden himself, and I understood. I let it go too far. I knew better, but"—she lifted one shoulder, darted a quick, unhappy glance from Sonny to me, and finished—"like I said, that's no excuse."

She was silent for a moment, playing with her fork.

Then she added, "Now I'm a material witness in a criminal investigation. Until the trial, I can't change my address. But after that . . . My parents live in Arizona. I thought Ringo and I might try our luck out there."

Sonny smiled. "I'm sure there's a great need for dancing dogs there."

Sandy returned her smile bravely. "And maybe even physical therapists."

The man called Alan Mesner had been picked up less than ten miles from town. He now awaited trial in the county jail on charges of parole violation, kidnapping, aggravated assault, conspiracy to commit murder, attempted murder, and that was only the beginning of the list.

Charges were pending, I understood, against David Kines, who, according to Mesner, had hired him to "mess up" Leo White. Mickey White had made Mesner a better offer—a half million in gold coins and he didn't even have to get his hands dirty. All he had to do was meet her at the cabin with the gun and collect a bag filled with gold.

Mickey had set up everything, the fake e-mails from Sandy arranging the tryst, the isolated cabin in the woods, even the missing dog food so that Leo would have to leave long enough for Alan to deliver the gun. It wasn't enough that her husband be punished for his infidelity; she wanted him to suffer for the rest of his life, even while she ended her own. She had known that, even if Leo should somehow escape prosecution for her murder, her father would exact his own revenge for her death.

The plan had gone awry when Leo, returning from town, had pulled around the back of the cabin, intending to enter through the back door. He had either seen his dead wife through the back window, or he had seen Mesner coming out the front and had recognized him as the man who had previously stalked him; no one could know for sure. At any rate, he took flight, and Mesner, whose vehicle was hidden in the brush off the road a few hundred yards, lost enough time in the chase that he never had a chance of catching Leo. In his panic, Leo drove down a ravine and suffered a head injury that eventually caused him to pass out and drown in the creek.

Pending investigation, the police had kept the discovery of the bag of money quiet, so Mesner had never known that it was all over. With no chance of getting the money from Leo, he had waited for Sandy, certain that she either already had it or knew where it was. Sandy had not even known Leo was dead until Mesner told her.

Sonny inquired, "Are they still treating Mickey White's death as a murder? Does anybody believe that story about her killing herself?"

I shrugged. "My sources at the sheriff's department have dried up. All I know is that the district attorney hasn't charged Mesner with murder. That makes me think he doesn't have enough evidence."

"I believe it," Sandy said. "Mickey White was a strange and cruel woman. I think it's completely within her character to plot her own suicide just to punish her husband."

I saw the shadow fall over her bruised face and noticed the mostly uneaten lunch. I said, "Come on, this is supposed to be a party. Let's talk about something else."

And so we did. We talked about Hero, who in his now unofficial capacity as a service dog, lay quietly but alertly under the table near Sonny's feet awaiting his next command. On hearing of Sonny's predicament, and learning that I was more than willing to take whatever time was needed to help rehabilitate Hero, Wes Richards had expedited the paperwork, making it possible for Sonny to adopt Hero as a retired service dog.

Even if Hero never fully recovered from his terror of loud noises, he was more than capable of meeting Sonny's needs. She would never again have to worry about falling and being unable to reach the phone, and the steps that Hero could save her each day doing ordinary things like carrying laundry to the hamper and picking up things she had dropped would give her many pain-free hours she might not otherwise have had.

Almost more important, Hero was working again. He walked with pride and energy in his step and, when he was off duty, even ran and played with Mystery—although he never got so far away from Sonny that he could not hear if she called, or see her if she needed him. Sonny said that saving us from the fire had, in his mind, made up in some fashion for being unable to save Mickey. I don't know about that, but I do know a happy dog when I see one. And Hero's spirit had been restored.

We talked too, about dancing dogs, and how eager Cisco was to start adding a dance routine to his therapy dog visits at the nursing home as soon as he was back on all four paws. By the time Sandy left to pick up Ringo and check out of the hotel for her trip back to Charleston, she was laughing and promising to send me some instructional videos as soon as she got home. She was almost, but not quite, the vivacious young woman I had met at the Pet Fair a week ago. And although she might never be that carefree again, I thought some of the pall that surrounded her was beginning to lift.

When we were alone, Sonny said, reading my thoughts, "She'll be dancing again in no time."

"I hope so." I picked up my coffee cup. "Thanks for lunch. This was a good idea."

"I hope this doesn't spoil the party, but . . ." Sonny reached into her oversized purse and took out a manila envelope. "I was in Asheville yesterday and saw Paul Kelly. He asked me to bring you these."

Sonny was not a divorce lawyer, but she knew someone who was. His name was Paul Kelly. I took the envelope from her slowly.

"There's no hurry," she said. "Take them home, look them over, call Paul with any questions. You can mail them, or I'll take them back with me."

I opened the envelope and slid out the legal document. At the top of the first page was written PETITION FOR DIVORCE.

"When are you going to see him again?" I asked casually.

"I'm going in that direction tomorrow. But that doesn't mean—"

"Don't be silly." I took a pen from my purse and quickly scrawled my signature on all the lines where a tabbed yellow arrow said SIGN HERE. "No point in

wasting the postage. Besides"—I returned the papers to
the envelope and slid it back across the table to her. I knew
my smile was sad, and a little forced, but at least it was
a smile—"it's not as though I haven't done this before."

She nodded, understanding, and put the envelope
back into her purse.

We finished our coffee, chatting in a desultory fashion, and then she glanced at the cashier's stand. "It looks
like the lunch crowd has thinned out. I'm going to let
Hero practice paying the check. Actually," she added,
using her cane to help steady herself as she got to her
feet. The minute she touched the cane, Hero was standing and alert. "Hero knows exactly what he's doing. I'm
the one who needs the practice!"

I watched, grinning with pleasure, as Hero took the
bill from Sonny's hand and carried it to the counter. All
the waitresses gathered around, oohing and aahing, as he
placed his front paws on the counter and waited for
change.

A soft voice said my name, and I looked up. My grin
faded as I saw Wyn standing there.

She gestured hesitantly to the seat Sonny had just va-
cated. "Could I—? I'll only take a minute, I promise."

Because my mother had raised me to have impeccable
manners, even though I did not always use them, I said,
"Of course. But I was just getting ready to leave."

"Please." She slid into the seat opposite me. "A
minute, I promise."

It was odd, seeing her out of uniform. I know I must
have before, but I had never noticed what a pretty girl
she was, with her curly, shoulder-length, honey-colored

hair and a figure that looked nice in the turtleneck sweater and fitted jeans she wore today. It was just odd, looking at her in a whole new light.

She folded her hands tightly on the table before her and said, glancing down at them, "I just wanted to you know . . . I'm leaving."

"The department?" That did not surprise me.

She nodded. "And town."

That did.

She said, "With your uncle retiring, Buck will run for sheriff next year. I think it would be easier for him if I weren't here. I got a job in Cantwell, working security at the electronics plant. It's a forty-five-minute commute, and there's no point in my making it twice a day until we . . . well, until we know what we're going to do."

Now I was confused. "We?"

She nodded. Color rose in her cheeks and I knew it took a lot of courage for her to meet my eyes. "Buck and me. That's the other thing I want to tell you—to make sure you understood," she went on in a rush. "What happened—it wasn't what you think, at least not entirely. I took the job in Cantwell before—well, before, because I knew I couldn't keep working with Buck feeling the way I did about him. I knew he was trying to work things out with you. But then, when I told him I was quitting the department, and leaving town . . . things changed." She drew a breath. "A lot of things."

I said, fumbling for my purse, "I really have to—"

But she held my gaze firmly. "I wanted you to know he didn't cheat on you, and that I didn't try to steal him away from you. It was only after you had broken up that we—well, talked about our feelings."

I was suffused with a sudden wave of sympathy. It was irrational, but in light of everything else that had happened, it seemed almost inevitable. "Wyn, I'm not mad at you," I said gently. "I don't blame you."

She held up a quick, staying hand. "I know he has a reputation," she said. "I know he's still trying to get over you, and I know that maybe he never will. And the thing is, I can deal with that. You two have a history that no one else can compete with, and I understand that, and respect it. But for now, until something happens to change my mind, I want to try with him." Another breath. "We both want to try. We want to give this our best shot, and see what happens. I wanted you to know that."

We sat there in silence for a moment or two while I tried to process what I had heard, and to make sense of it. I couldn't think of a single thing to say.

She stood. "Well," she said. "Good-bye, Raine."

I said, still a little dazed, "Good-bye."

And then I added, "I hope things work out for you, Wyn."

She looked back at me and smiled. "Thanks," she said.

And to my very great surprise, I realized that I actually meant it.

It was after nine one evening a few days later when I saw the flash of headlights on my window. The dogs were all in bed—the girls crated, and Cisco, who had only recently been allowed to climb the stairs again, was no doubt snoozing on my bed. I had banked the fire in the fireplace and was just getting ready to turn out the lights and go upstairs myself.

I went quickly to the window and watched the man get out of the car and climb my steps. Before he could ring the doorbell and wake the dogs, I hurried to open the door.

"Good evening, Miss Stockton," said Miles Young. He was holding in his hand a package with an elaborate gold bow. "Is Cisco at home?"

I looked at him skeptically, blocking the narrow opening of the door with my body to keep out the cold. "He's asleep."

"Oh." He sounded disappointed. Then he said, "I understand you've had quite a bit of excitement around here."

"Some."

"I'm sorry I missed it. I was called to Istanbul."

"You were not."

"Swear to God."

"What do you want?"

"I thought I'd send a crew down here with a front-end loader in the morning to get started clearing out some of the rubble from the kennel fire, if it's okay with you. I didn't want the heavy equipment to wake you."

I scowled at him. "Don't do me any favors."

"I'm not. You'll be paying them the going rate."

I hesitated. "Well, in that case . . ."

"Good."

I said, "I'm sorry I accused you of shooting Cisco. I was wrong."

"So you were."

That was not the most gracious acceptance of an apology I had ever heard. But then, perhaps I could have been more gracious in delivering it.

I added, a little grudgingly, "Thanks for the new animal shelter."

He smiled. "Just trying to make friends in high places."

I was getting cold, and I rubbed one furry-slipper-covered foot against the other to illustrate the fact. "Is there anything else?"

He held out the package to me. "If you would be good enough to deliver this to Cisco, with my best wishes for a speedy recovery."

I took the fancily wrapped box hesitantly, gave him a cautious, studious look, and then carefully lifted the lid. Inside, each one nestled in its own velvet-lined, custom-molded cup, were a dozen gourmet dog biscuits, individually wrapped in gold foil.

I tried not to smile. I really did. But I couldn't help it. I looked at Miles Young for a long moment, standing there on my porch in the dark and cold, and then I opened the door wider and invited him in.

Change can sneak up on you sometimes, knock you flat, bowl you over. Sometimes there's just no point in fighting it.

And sometimes it's not such a bad thing.

DONNA BALL

RAPID FIRE

A Raine Stockton Dog Mystery

With her kennel business and her part-time job with the forest service, Raine Stockton is having a hectic summer when the FBI drops in to see her about her old flame Andy Fontana. Fontana disappeared from her life when he was connected with an act of sabotage that left several people dead. Now, he's an eco-terrorist on the Ten Most Wanted list, and the feds think Raine can help them bring him to justice.

ALSO AVAILABLE
SMOKY MOUNTAIN TRACKS

"DONNA BALL...KNOWS HOW TO WRITE A PAGE TURNER."
—BEVERLY CONNOR

Available wherever books are sold or at
penguin.com